Dear Reader,

We have exciting news! Starting in January, the Harlequin Blaze books you know and love will be getting a brand-new look. And it's *hot!* Turn to the back of this book for a sneak peek....

But don't worry—nothing else about the Blaze books has changed. You'll still find those unforgettable love stories with intrepid heroines, hot, hunky heroes and a double dose of sizzle!

So be sure to check out our new supersexy covers. You'll find these newly packaged Blaze editions on the shelves December 18th, 2012, wherever you buy your books.

In the meantime, check out this month's red-hot reads.

LET IT SNOW by Leslie Kelly and Jennifer LaBrecque
(A Blazing Bedtime Stories Holiday Edition)

HIS FIRST NOELLE by Rhonda Nelson
(Men Out of Uniform)

ON A SNOWY CHRISTMAS NIGHT by Debbi Rawlins
(Made in Montana)

NICE & NAUGHTY by Tawny Weber

ALL I WANT FOR CHRISTMAS
by Lori Wilde, Kathleen O'Reilly and Candace Havens
(A Sizzling Yuletide Anthology)

HERS FOR THE HOLIDAYS by Samantha Hunter
(The Berringers)

Happy holidays!

Brenda Chin
Senior Editor
Harlequin Blaze

ABOUT THE AUTHORS

Lori Wilde is a *New York Times* bestselling author and has written more than forty books. She's been nominated for a RITA® Award and four *RT Book Reviews* Reviewers' Choice Awards. Her books have been excerpted in *Cosmopolitan, Redbook* and *Quick & Simple.* Lori teaches writing online through Ed2go. She's also an RN trained in forensics and she volunteers at a women's shelter. Visit her website at www.loriwilde.com.

Kathleen O'Reilly wrote her first romance at the age of eleven, which to her undying embarrassment was read aloud to her class. Now she is an award-winning author of nearly twenty romances published in countries all over the world. Kathleen lives in New York with her husband and their two children, who outwit her daily.

Award-winning author and columnist **Candace "Candy" Havens** lives in Texas with her mostly understanding husband, two children and two dogs, Scoobie and Gizmo. Candy is a nationally syndicated entertainment columnist for FYI Television. She has interviewed just about everyone in Hollywood from George Clooney and Orlando Bloom to Nicole Kidman and Kate Beckinsale. Her popular online writers' workshop has more than thirteen hundred students and provides free classes to professional and aspiring writers.

Lori Wilde
Kathleen O'Reilly
Candace Havens

ALL I WANT FOR CHRISTMAS...

HARLEQUIN®
entertain, enrich, inspire™

ISBN-13: 978-0-373-79731-8

ALL I WANT FOR CHRISTMAS...

Copyright © 2012 by Harlequin Books S.A.

The publisher acknowledges the copyright holders of the individual works as follows:

CHISTMAS KISSES
Copyright © 2012 by Lori Vanzura

BARING IT ALL
Copyright © 2012 by Kathleen Panov

A HOT DECEMBER NIGHT
Copyright © 2012 by Candace Havens

Recycling programs for this product may not exist in your area.

This edition published by arrangement with Harlequin Books S.A.

For questions and comments about the quality of this book, please contact us at CustomerService@Harlequin.com.

® and TM are trademarks of Harlequin Enterprises Limited or its corporate affiliates. Trademarks indicated with ® are registered in the United States Patent and Trademark Office, the Canadian Trade Marks Office and in other countries.

www.Harlequin.com

Printed in U.S.A.

CONTENTS

LORI WILDE

CHRISTMAS KISSES

To Kathleen and Candace.
It's been a pleasure writing this anthology with you.

1

HANDS ON HIS hips, Police Sergeant Noah Briscoe, head of the general investigations unit, stared at the smoldering rubble of what was once the number-one historical landmark in Pine Crest, Virginia. The mansion home of Colin T. Price, arguably the most beloved governor who ever held the state's office, and visited by over half a million tourists a year.

The acrid stench assaulted Noah with dark memories that he impatiently shoved aside. No. He would not go there.

But how did he block out the past when charred metal thrust up from the smoldering heap like blackened bones, taunted him, reminding him of another burned house, another injured woman, another ruined Christmas?

When the call came in, Noah had been at a twenty-four-hour gym, working out his frustrations. Lately, he'd had trouble sleeping and it had a lot to do with the stress of the holiday season. Crime went up in November and December. Robbery, shoplifting, domestic abuse. Something about the holidays riled people. If it were up to Noah, he'd outlaw the whole damn thing.

But there was a secondary reason he hadn't been able to sleep. Sexual frustration. He hadn't had sex in almost a year and he seriously needed it bad. There was only so much exercising a man could do, after all.

And whenever he thought of sex, he thought of Alana O'Hara, the fiery, redheaded defense attorney he'd almost talked into bed this past summer, before common sense prevailed. They'd flirted for weeks, shared a deep wet tongue kiss in her office and gone out on exactly one date.

At the end of the evening, after they took the making out far past second base in the back seat of his SUV, Alana had chickened out, telling him that while there was no denying the sexual chemistry, they just weren't compatible.

She was right.

They were oil and water, but hot damn that woman was something else. Great body, mind like a steel trap, strong opinions she wasn't afraid to voice. Noah suppressed a smile.

Thinking of Alana had the desired effect. It got his mind off those disturbing Christmas memories.

Now, refocus. Task at hand.

The arson investigator, Bic Beckham, was poking around in the ashes. Crime scene technicians snapped photographs. Firefighters moved to and fro. Noah's men were busy stringing out yellow crime-scene tape and setting up portable floodlights to aid the investigation and keeping the lookie-loos at bay behind sawhorse barricades.

An ambulance sat at the curb, strobes flashing red into the night as the paramedics loaded up the unidentified, unconscious woman who'd been found in the foyer of the mansion. She'd been overcome by smoke inhalation before she could reach the door.

Which raised the questions, who was she and what had she been doing in the mansion after hours?

After Noah finished here, he would follow the ambulance to the hospital to check on her condition. If she died, this would become a murder investigation and Homicide would take over.

"Briscoe." Bic beckoned with a crook of his finger. "C'mere."

Gingerly, Noah picked his way around puddles of water and hot debris to where Bic stood beside a pile of crumpled bricks that had previously been one of the mansion's four fireplace chimneys. "Whatcha got?"

"See here." Bic pointed to a thin blackened triangular mark seared into the brick paving stones that surrounded the toppled fireplace.

A very narrow V-shape char pattern was indicative of a fire that burned hotter than normal. Say, for instance, one that had been assisted by an accelerant. Noah ran a palm over his whisker-roughened chin.

"I'll know more when the embers cool and we can start sifting through the ashes," Bic said. "But between this and what the firefighters observed of the fire's behavior, it looks like we've got a case of arson on our hands."

Arson.

Noah raked fingers through his hair. Who would want to burn down the town's biggest tourist attraction, and why?

Bic returned to his work. Noah called his men over, told them it was suspected arson. Most arsonists had a need to watch the fire they'd set and that was often how they were caught. "Anybody among those rubberneckers strike you as suspicious?"

"You mean besides Santa?" asked Jimmy Thornton, an earnest-faced, wet-behind-the-ears rookie.

Santa?

Noah's gaze shifted in the direction Jimmy indicated. Sure enough, there was a man in a Santa suit standing in the middle of the crowd. Noah's gaze locked with the blue-eyed man of indeterminate age.

Santa held his stare, and inexplicably, Noah felt a chill pass straight through his bones. Was it just his aversion to all things Noel? Or was his gut trying to tell him something?

"Go find out who he is," Noah told Jimmy.

"You don't really think Santa is the arsonist, do you?"

Naive kid. Noah cocked an eyebrow, drilled him with a hard look. "You never heard of *Bad Santa?* He's not above breaking the law just because he's wearing a Santa suit."

Jimmy flushed. Looked embarrassed. Not so many years ago, the young rookie was hanging his stocking on the fireplace mantel. Hell, he probably still did.

"Thornton." Noah jerked his head in the direction of the chubby guy in red. "There's no such thing as Santa Claus. Get on it."

"I'm going, Sarg." Jimmy hustled off.

"Scrooge."

Noah turned to see Bic grinning at him. "Not you, too."

"Oh, I'm fully aware that arsonists come in all shapes, sizes, ages and outfits," Bic said. "But seriously, why would the guy commit arson while wearing a Santa suit? Too restrictive. Attracts too much attention. Not too mention he'd get soot all over himself."

"And then he could just say it's from sliding down a chimney. Perfect excuse."

Bic laughed and went back to what he was doing. Noah circled around to the front of the building, which was still largely intact. The foyer was where the first responders had found the unconscious mystery woman. She hadn't had any identification on her person, but maybe she'd had a purse. He touched the doorknob. It was cold.

He pushed open the door. Unlike the rest of the house, this area had less debris. Water from the firemen's diligent soaking dripped and splattered all around him.

Noah squatted, pulled a flashlight from his jacket pocket

and shone it over the foyer floor. The heat had buckled the old mahogany wood. What a shame. He shook his head, ran the beam over the charred Persian rug that delineated the foyer from the parlor. His mother had brought him here on a Christmas tour when he was a kid. She'd loved both history and the holidays.

Dammit, there were those old memories again. It had been twenty years, but Christmas was a bitch, and now with the fire destroying the mansion it was inevitable he'd think about that *other* fire.

He scrubbed a palm down his face. What was going on? He'd made peace with his past long ago. Why had he been thinking about it lately?

Stop it. Pull out some of your X-rated daydreams of Alana O'Hara. Remember the one where she's dressed up in thigh-high black leather boots and a little red bikini?

Noah smiled at the visual. Their relationship might never have gotten off the ground, but Alana was a big help when he needed to redirect his attention. Just thinking about those million-mile-long legs and that full head of lush auburn hair—

Something glinted in the beam of his flashlight. Wait a minute. What was that? His brain caught up with his eyes and he realized what he was seeing.

A gold belt buckle attached to a long, four-inch-wide black belt. The belt was large enough to encircle at least a forty-four-inch waist.

He straightened, took a pair of rubber gloves from his pocket and then leaned over to carefully lift a curl of blackened wallpaper that draped over the belt. It looked exactly like the sort of belt Santa Claus might wear. What was it doing here in the foyer of the Price Mansion?

Contrary to what television would have people believe, only fifteen percent of all arson cases were ever solved. Could he have gotten lucky right off the bat?

Noah peeled off the gloves, went outside and called to one of the crime scene techs to come photograph the evidence before bagging and tagging it. He scanned the crowd, searching for Santa or the rookie Jimmy Thornton, but saw neither.

Another one of his officers approached. "Sarg, we got a witness."

"Who?"

The officer consulted his tablet computer. "Agnes Gaines. Lives next door."

"Where is she?"

The officer indicated an elderly birdlike woman positioned behind the nearest sawhorse.

"Bring her over," Noah instructed.

The officer assisted the woman around the barricade. She was thin as a licorice whip with a tidy cap of snow-white hair. She wore a man's peacoat thrown over pajamas and house slippers. A pair of oversized glasses made her brown eyes appeared owlish.

"What did you see, Mrs. Gaines?"

"Miss Gaines," she corrected. "I never married."

"You saw something?" he asked, guiding her back to the topic at hand.

She nodded. "I couldn't sleep and I got up to make myself a glass of warm milk."

"What time was this?"

"Hmm, around eleven-thirty."

Noah glanced at his watch. It was 2:00 a.m. now. "What did you see?"

"I happened to notice the full moon shining through my kitchen window. I love a full moon, so I stepped out on the back porch for a good look."

He wanted to tell her to cut to the chase, Reader's Digest version, but he forced himself to be patient. Active listening was an essential tool in a good police officer's arsenal. "Yes, ma'am."

"The moon was hanging right over the Price Mansion, such an elegant old structure. Such a shame." She shook her head.

Noah cleared his throat.

"I'm digressing, aren't I? Well, the moon was shining brightly and I saw the front door of the mansion open. I was paying close attention because there were no lights on inside and the building closes to the public at five, so there shouldn't be anyone in there. I was thinking it might be prankster kids. Then the door opens up and guess who struts out?"

"I have no idea, ma'am."

"I'm being coy, aren't I? Excuse me, Officer, it's a bad habit of mine. I was a high school drama teacher for forty-two years."

Noah shifted his weight, leaned forward and stared at her hard. "Yes, ma'am."

"Are you going to guess?"

"Santa Claus."

Her mouth puckered in disappointment. "How did you know?"

"Lucky guess." He flicked his gaze to the patrol officer who'd brought Agnes over. "Walk Miss Gaines home."

"Yes, sir." The officer extended his arm to the witness. "This way, ma'am."

Santa Claus in the crowd. The belt from a Santa costume found in the foyer. And an eyewitness who placed a man in a Santa suit exiting the mansion just before the blaze started.

Ho, ho, ho. Merry fricking Christmas.

Jolly Saint Nick had just become Noah's number-one suspect.

ALANA O'HARA WAS having one sizzling sex dream, featuring none other than the extremely virile Sergeant Noah Briscoe, when her ringing cell phone woke her just when they were getting to the good part.

She bolted upright, feeling hot and achy and frustrated. Why did she keep having erotic dreams about the man? It had been months since the date that had ended with a heavy petting session and the consensus that a relationship between them was untenable. She should have forgotten all about him by now.

Apparently, her subconscious had not. It was the third time this week she'd dreamed of Noah.

Maybe she should have just had sex with him and gotten him out of her system. She had to admit, he'd been a fabulous kisser and the things he could with his fingers....

She blew out a breath. *Pure magic.*

The phone rang again. She snagged it up. It was her boss, Dwight Jacoby.

"Got a public defender case for you," he said.

Of course. Those were the only solo cases she got. Unlike the majority of jurisdictions, Pine Crest did not have a public defender's office. Instead, they used a panel of private law firms for those defendants who could not afford their own counsel. The firms operated as contractors and received fixed compensation from government coffers. Junior members of the law firms cut their teeth on such cases. "Yes, sir. What's the crime?" She tossed back the covers, got out of bed. Phone calls at three in the morning were part of the drill. As she talked, she stripped off her pajama bottoms and stepped into the skirt she'd worn the day before.

"Arson. Price Mansion."

"You're kidding. The Price Mansion burned?"

"Yep."

"Ahh, that's a crying shame. I loved that place."

"It is a town icon."

"Who's the accused?"

Dwight snorted. "This is the good part."

She slipped an arm from one sleeve of her pajama top, transferred the phone to the other ear and eased her other arm out, as well. "What's so funny?"

"Santa Claus."

"What about Santa Claus?"

"Apparently, he's the firebug."

"No. Really?" In the darkness, she pulled open the bureau drawer, found her bra and wriggled into it. She hated hearing this. Alana adored Christmas. It was her absolute favorite time of year.

"Real name is…get this…Christopher Clausen. He works at the Pine Crest Mall, denies he started the fire even though they've got circumstantial evidence that proves otherwise and he's claiming he actually *is* Santa Claus. It's why I assigned you to the case. You've got that wide-eyed Christmas spirit."

"Why do I feel like I've stepped into a remake of *Miracle on 34th Street?*"

"Because you have." Dwight laughed. "Get down to the police station. They've got him in interrogation room two and they're waiting on you."

Fifteen minutes later, sans makeup, Alana knocked on the door of interrogation room two at the Pine Crest Police Department. The door opened and she found herself staring into a pair of sharp brown eyes.

Unnerved, her gaze slid past a rumpled, light blue buttondown shirt with the sleeves rolled up revealing tanned forearms, on down to long lean legs encased in black trousers and finally to a pair of new leather shoes that clearly had been tramping around a fire site.

Soot.

She could smell the smoke on his clothes. Quickly, she darted a glance back at his face, wishing she'd taken the extra five minutes to put on some mascara, lipstick and blush.

No wonder she kept having sex dreams about him. He exuded a primal male energy that tugged low in her belly.

Noah Briscoe.

She knew he'd been up all night investigating the fire, but he looked alert and wide-awake, staring at her with that intense, cynical stare of his. Even so, there was an inner calmness about him that appealed to her. She came from a boisterous, argumentative family of mostly attorneys and judges who could debate either side of any issue. Noah was a man of singular convictions. Right and wrong. Black and white. While her world was totally gray. Complex and complicated.

Was that part of the attraction? The delineated simplicity of him?

"I'm Mr. Clausen's court-appointed counsel," she announced.

Noah sized her up with an appreciative glance, his gaze moving from her eyes to her lips and on down her body. Everywhere his gaze roamed she heated up.

Then he took a step closer and reached out and touched her sweater over her heart.

Startled, Alana jerked back.

"Let's not feed into his delusion," Noah said.

It was only then that she realized she wore a Santa Claus pin on her sweater. "Oh." She blinked. "Oh."

Smoothly, Noah bent his head, found the pin clasp and unhooked it. His knuckles grazed just over her breast.

She stopped breathing.

He stepped back, extended his hand. She held out her palm and he dropped the Santa pin into it. His masculine potency reminded her why she'd called things off between them. With his sarcastic wit, dark outlook and drop-dead gorgeous body, he'd simply been too much for her to handle.

"I'm not delusional," said the man handcuffed to the interrogation table. "I'm the real deal."

For the first time, Alana noticed her client.

He was dressed in full Santa regalia. She couldn't pinpoint his age. He was past middle-age, but not elderly. He possessed a robust figure, twinkling blue eyes, rosy cheeks and a genuine smile beneath a thick white beard. Red suit and hat with furry white collar and cuffs, black boots, white gloves. The only thing missing from the outfit was a wide black belt.

"Hello, Mr. Clausen," she said, "My name is Alana O'Hara."

"The spirit of Christmas." Clausen smiled.

"Excuse me?"

"That's about all he'll say," Noah supplied. "Now that you're here, I'm hoping we'll get somewhere."

"What are the charges?"

Noah told her. She hadn't heard about the woman injured in the fire. That added a whole new wrinkle to the arson case. Santa was in deep trouble.

Noah spent the next fifteen minutes questioning Christopher Clausen. For the most part, Alana told her client not to answer. On the surface, he appeared open and honest and fully willing to cooperate. The only problem was, he kept insisting he was Santa Claus.

"Mr. Clausen, do you have an explanation for how your belt got into the foyer of the Price Mansion?" Noah quizzed.

Alana rested a hand on her client's forearm. "You don't have to answer that." She met Noah's hard-edged stare and got to her feet. "It's time to terminate this interview, Sergeant Briscoe. I need to consult with my client in private."

A sardonic look crossed his face. His default expression. Erect that barrier. Don the tough-guy mask. She'd gotten a glimpse beyond that, however, and although she had not unearthed the full story, she sensed a bone-deep vulnerability that he never showed anyone.

His teeth flashed, white and straight. It was a cool smile with something hot simmering beneath. "Sure, whatever you *need,* Ms. O'Hara."

Was it her imagination or had he put added emphasis on the word need? She thought about her sex dream, felt a flush of heat rise to her cheeks. He noticed and his smile widened, went wicked. She didn't trust an accommodating cop. Why was he being so accommodating?

Sergeant Briscoe. Ms. O'Hara. They were being all formal, as if they hadn't once had a sweet tussle in the back of his SUV.

He got up, walked to the door, nodded to a guard standing outside. "You can take Mr. Clausen to lockup."

The guard entered. Removed Christopher Clausen. Left Noah and Alana alone in the interrogation room.

His hot gaze was on her again. They were both standing. He was closer to the door than she was. "Santa's guilty as sin."

"Love the rush to judgment. It's so you."

His eyes narrowed but she could have swore he was suppressing an amused smile. "We've got an eyewitness who saw him leave the mansion just before the fire broke out. A black belt was found in the foyer and he's missing one from his Santa suit. Clausen was in the crowd watching the place burn." Noah ticked off the evidence on his fingers.

"Every bit of it circumstantial."

"Circumstantial evidence gets a bad rap. You know as well as I do that it's enough for a conviction."

"I know you're hardnosed, Briscoe, but I had no idea you were closed-minded as well."

"Your guy is a nut case."

"He's a bit unconventional, but that doesn't make him crazy."

"He thinks he's Santa Claus."

"I don't think he means that literally. It's more spirit of Christmas thing. As in, *Yes Virginia, there is a Santa Claus.*"

"Cute. Considering we're in Virginia."

"That's what I'm getting at. Clausen is just trying to prove a point." Alana was talking out of her hat here. She knew it and Briscoe knew it. She had no idea whether Clausen had a psychological disorder or not, but she was his defense attorney. It was up to her to defend him.

"Which is?" Noah's gaze drilled into hers and he crossed his arms over his chest. Another barrier along with the challenging tone.

His proximity did something curious to her nerve endings. More specifically, the nerve endings in a certain region of her body that hadn't been touched by a man in a long time. She notched her chin up. "The spirit of Christmas resides in everyone. Even you, Scrooge."

He laughed, loud and startling. "Let me guess, your favorite movie in the whole wide world is *Miracle on 34th Street.*"

Nailed it. Completely.

She wasn't going to let him know. She held his stare. What she saw there made her forget all about Christopher Clausen and the burned-out Price Mansion.

Raw desire.

Desire that matched her own.

"What's Clausen's motive?" she asked, determined to ignore what she saw written on his face. "He doesn't have a motive for burning down the Price Mansion."

Noah shrugged. "Maybe Santa is just a plain old firebug who gets his sexual jollies from setting fires?"

Her breath was coming in shallow little puffs of air. Now she remembered the real reason she'd pulled the plug on their budding romance. Noah was too much man for her. If she ever slept with him, she knew she'd fall head over heels and that was a risk she simply could not take. She was just getting started in her career. She wasn't ready for anything serious. A casual fling was all she wanted.

But one thing was abundantly clear.

There was nothing casual about Noah Briscoe.

2

NOAH LEFT THE station around 10:00 a.m., headed home to snatch a quick nap. Alana's words circled his brain. *I know you're hard-nosed, Briscoe, but I had no idea you were closed-minded as well.*

Was he closed-minded?

Noah didn't think so. The evidence against crazy Clausen was as clear-cut as the aged pastrami on the Reuben sandwiches at Mac's Diner. Sliced, hot and ready to serve.

Not closed-minded, eh? You're thinking Clausen is crazy when you have no solid proof of any mental disorder. Other than an enchantment with Christmas. If he locked people up for excess Christmas spirit the Pine Crest jail would be full to the ceiling and chief among his prisoners would be Alana herself.

How was it that Alana's offhand comments could embed themselves so firmly in his head and cause a twinge of doubt? For the most part, he was a self-confident man. But she had a way of rattling his cage when he least expected it.

Noah had no sooner passed through the back entrance into the employee parking lot, surrounded by an eight-foot chain-link fence and liberally posted with security cameras, than he spied the protesters marching the sidewalk outside the locked gate. They were chanting and carrying picket signs reading: *Free Santa!* and *Pine Crest Police Department ruins Christmas.*

A van from the local TV station sat parked at the curb and the amused camera crew filmed both the protesters and Noah as he slid behind the wheel of his black SUV. He slammed the door closed, sighed and rolled his eyes. Who had leaked Clausen's arrest to the media so quickly?

Alana?

He immediately dismissed the thought. She might be full of the Christmas spirit, but she wouldn't pull something so underhanded.

Would she?

She was an eager young lawyer looking to prove herself. Noah's suspicious nature kicked up. He'd learned a long time ago that it was a good idea not to trust anyone too much.

He drove from the lot, past the protesters and news media, headed home to his empty apartment. He'd promised himself he was going to buy a house. With the interest rates so low and a hefty down payment in the bank, there was really no reason not to take that next step. But he had no wife, no girlfriend, not even a pet. There was no need to rush into home ownership, but he was tired of apartment renting. Nothing permanent. Nothing that belonged to him. Strange. Until recently, those had been the positive points of renting. When had his thinking started to shift?

The air smelled of snow as he trudged up the steps. This time of year brought out the worst in him. He wished he could take a vacation, head for the Bahamas. But in all honesty, he wasn't a beachy kind of guy. His ideal vacation involved an isolated cabin in Montana and plenty of fly-fishing. Wrong time of year for that.

Once inside, he stripped off his clothes and got into the shower, scrubbing the soot and wood smoke smell from his skin. He thought of Alana and the sleepy-eyed, just-rolled-out-of-the-sheets look she'd worn to the interrogation room.

He got hard instantly, cursed himself under his breath and dealt with it in the most efficient way possible. Afterward, he toweled himself dry and fell naked into bed, determined to dream of nothing.

Noah woke from his nap sometime later, feeling foggy and ravenous. It was five-thirty in the evening. He hadn't intended to sleep that long. His stomach grumbled. Groggily, he stumbled to the kitchen, opened the refrigerator door and peered in.

A bottle of ketchup, another of Dijon mustard, maple syrup, Spanish olives, six-pack of beer and half a carton of milk. He opened up the milk, took a whiff. Ugh. Poured it down the sink.

The pantry was just as sparse. A tin of sardines, but no crackers. Froot Loops. Barbecue potato chips with mostly crumbs left. Cans of corn, green beans and spinach. The search of the freezer yielded a stack of TV dinners, but his microwave was on the fritz, and way in the back, he found a forgotten container of rocky road ice cream coated with ice crystals.

Sighing, he shut the freezer and went to get dressed. Not long after, he was sitting in the booth at Mac's Diner, close to the station house. The big-screen TV mounted on the wall above the front counter was playing the evening news.

The image of a pretty reporter on the courthouse steps popped onto the screen. Microphone in hand, the reporter smiled into the camera. Around her protestors carried *Free Santa!* picket signs. That was still going on? Noah rolled his eyes.

"Maxie Marks here, reporting for KPCV. It's been a lively day at City Hall as Christopher Clausen supporters turned out in droves to demand the release of Santa Claus, who stands accused of burning down the Price Mansion," said the reporter in an über-perky voice. "This afternoon, Judge Kline granted his lawyer's shockingly low bail request of ten thousand dollars. Clausen, who's known around town as the Spirit of Christmas, is out on bond and free to return to his job as Santa at the Pine Crest Mall. Look, here comes Clausen's lawyer now. Let's see if we can get a statement."

The reporter and her camera crew sprinted higher up the courthouse steps. Noah straightened, watched the screen for Alana. She ought to be pretty proud of herself for swinging such a low bail.

But instead of Alana, the reporter thrust her microphone into the face of Dwight Jacoby, one of the most renowned defense attorneys in the state. What was a big cheese like Jacoby doing on a small-potatoes case like this? And what had happened to Alana? She should have been giving the interview.

Just then the door to the diner flew open, bringing in a brisk gust of cold December wind and a striking redhead bundled up in a wool, houndstooth coat. Her head was down. Mumbling to herself, she stormed into the booth next to Noah, plucking off her gloves as she went. She doffed a white tam that matched her scarf and tossed it on the seat beside her. Running a hand through hair that crackled with static electricity, she finally glanced up.

Alana. Looking sexy as hell with a disgruntled scowl on her face.

Memories of the wee hours of the morning with Alana standing in his interrogation room, arguing with him every step of the way, rushed back to Noah.

"Oh, crap," she muttered, plenty loud enough for him to hear. "It's you."

Noah got up, sauntered toward her. "Dining alone?"

"Yes. Go away."

He slid into the seat across from her.

"Didn't you hear that last part? I said go away?"

"I heard you," he said mildly.

"You don't follow instructions well."

"A frequent fault of mine."

"So I've noticed."

"What's got you in a lather?" he asked.

She wanted to talk. It was written all over her. She was just uncertain about talking to him. "Stupid," she grumbled. "Stupid, stupid."

"Am I interrupting a private conversation?" He tried not to grin. She looked as if she'd get mad if he grinned.

"No. Yes." As she spoke, her words fanned the fine tendrils of red hair framing her face. "Go away."

"You're waffling."

A waitress popped over to their table. "What can I get you?"

"Reuben sandwich and coffee," Noah said, closing his menu at the same time Alana said, "He was just leaving."

Noah shook his head at the waitress. "I'm staying."

"Go away," Alana said succinctly. "I'm sick of men."

"I hear you on that one, honey," the waitress said.

Alana turned to the waitress. "What is it with guys? They give you the grunt work and then when you're enjoying it, they take it away from you."

"Pigs." The waitress tapped her chin with an index finger. "Swine. Greedy hogs." She shifted her gaze to Noah, narrowed her eyes. "You want me to call security to get rid of him for you?"

Noah smiled at Alana. "I'll buy your dinner if you let me stay."

"I'll call security," the waitress offered again. "It'll just take a second. Say the word."

"No, no," Alana said. "He's not the swine in question. At least not at the moment."

"Okay." The waitress twisted up her mouth, glared and pointed a finger at Noah. "I've got my eyes on you, buddy."

"Duly noted."

"Now," the waitress said to Alana, notepad in hand. "What'll you have?"

"Cobb salad, vinaigrette on the side, hot tea."

"Gotcha." She gave Noah one last glare and walked away.

"Why do I feel like I got caught in the middle of something?" he asked Alana.

"Because you brought your nosy butt over here."

"I was just concerned."

One skeptical eyebrow went up on her forehead. "Seriously?"

"Jacoby took the Clausen case away from you?"

She nodded. "He did."

Noah shrugged. "Protestors and media attention. It was inevitable."

"I was the one who negotiated the reduced bail for Clausen." She smoothed a paper napkin over her lap. "Jacoby gets all the credit."

"It's politics. Not to belittle your accomplishment or anything, but you got the bail lowered because Kline is up for reelection next year. He was kowtowing to public sentiment."

"You sound so philosophical. That's not the hotheaded Noah Briscoe I know. In fact, that's one of the reasons we never hooked up. You were so rigid—"

"I thought you liked that about me," he teased.

She ignored the innuendo. "And I was always trying to get you to be more fluid, see both sides of the issue. Now we've flip-flopped. What's happened?"

"Santa burned down the Price Mansion."

The waitress returned briefly to settle a cup of hot water and a tea bag at Alana's elbow, and a cup of coffee in front of Noah.

"Clausen didn't do it."

"The evidence says otherwise."

"You promised me that you'd keep investigating."

"What do you care now that Jacoby's hogging your case?"

"Justice. That's why."

He sat up straight. "We *have* flip-flopped. Usually, I'm the one caught on the justice prong and you're the one trying to see every side of an issue."

"Maybe our short association had an impact on our perspectives," she said, stirring sugar into her hot tea. "Imagine that."

"That's a scary thought."

She glanced up, teacup pressed to pursed lips gleaming with shiny red gloss, stream rising up against her smooth, creamy skin and curling the loose tendrils of auburn hair. Instantly, Noah found himself engulfed in another sexual fantasy. This must be what she looked like in a hot shower. The exotic water nymph. Holy Mother Nature.

"Terrifying," she agreed.

Noah gulped. He was in over his head. Which was the real reason they'd never gone on a second date. She had the power to change him and Noah did not like change.

But he knew her weakness. When the waitress brought their food, he told her, "Bring us a hot fudge sundae for dessert, extra fudge and two spoons."

The waitress shot a glance at Alana, waiting for her approval.

Alana looked like she was going to refuse, but then nodded. Ha! He had her. She was a sucker for chocolate. She gave him a furtive smile and made a soft noise so sensual, he got an erection.

"Maybe you should become a prosecutor, instead of a defense attorney," he said. "Considering your recent change in outlook."

"Everyone in my family is a judge or a defense attorney. We're big on the right to fair counsel."

"That doesn't preclude your being a prosecutor, does it?"

"I have an opinionated family."

"Afraid to be the black sheep, huh?"

She opened her mouth, shut it, opened it again and forked in a mouthful of lettuce, busied herself with chewing.

Controlling her tongue by keeping it busy? At the thought of her sexy little tongue, he grew even harder. He tackled his sandwich so he wouldn't have to watch those straight white teeth adeptly pluck a tomato from her fork.

"So," she said after a long moment. "What are your plans for Christmas?"

"Who, me?"

"You're the only one sitting here."

He shifted, dabbed at his mouth with a paper napkin, and cleared his throat. Was it a simple question, or was she angling for something more?

"Just making conversation," she said, reading his mind.

He shrugged. "Working."

"Do you work every Christmas?"

"Pretty much."

"Got something against the holiday?"

"More things than you can count."

Pity welled up in her eyes. "That's a shame."

"No it's not. I'm happy being a Grinch."

"No one is happy being a Grinch," she countered.

"I am," he replied staunchly. "And someone has to work the holidays. Crime doesn't stop simply because it's December 25th."

"So, no plans to attend the Pine Crest Firemen's Annual Christmas Eve Ball?"

Was she asking him out? That revved him up. "Um, isn't it usually held at the Price Mansion?"

"Yes."

"They're still having it?"

"Planning committee says yes, although they're scrambling to find a new location now that the mansion is no more." She pushed away her empty plate, picked up her tea. Her hands looked so delicate wrapped around the pink cup.

"I'm not much of a gala kind of guy."

The waitress stopped by to pick up their plates and drop off the gigantic hot fudge sundae. "Is he behaving himself?" she asked Alana.

"Surprisingly," Alana said, "yes."

"All right then." The waitress sailed off.

Alana's eyes lit up. "It's been forever since I had a hot fudge sundae."

"Dig in," Noah invited.

She picked up a spoon dipped into the ice cream, making sure to get plenty of gooey fudge. Going nuts for it just as Noah suspected she would. She took a bite, gave a throaty moan. "Mmm. Ooh, that is so good."

Noah's gaze fixed on her mouth as she nibbled fudge from her bottom lip. He liked how her face looked, blissed out and relaxed for the first time since coming into the diner. It made him relax. Smile.

"This is heaven." She sighed dreamily and took another bite.

He picked up the second spoon, dipped it into the sweet, sticky goo. For a long time they simply ate, the silence occasionally punctuated by Alana's rapturous sounds of appreciation. She closed her eyes, savoring every morsel. Never mind that his erection was solid concrete and she looked like she was about to have an orgasm at any second.

Mesmerized, Noah set down his spoon.

She opened one eye, caught him staring at her. "What is it?"

"You look…"

"What?"

No way in hell was he going to say what was on his mind. He shook his head.

Her other eye popped open. "Don't judge," she mumbled. "I had a bad day."

He held up both palms. "No judgment here."

"I normally never eat like this."

He eyed her smoking-hot body, couldn't stop the appreciative smile from crawling across his face. "Obviously."

She scooped up the last bite, turned the spoon around backward as she sucked off the fudgy ice cream with gung-ho gusto that cut right though him. She pondered him, spoon pressed against her lip. "What's your deal, Briscoe?"

"Deal?"

She dropped the spoon—licked completely clean—into the glass bowl. It made a clinking sound. "Why do you hate Christmas? Santa leave coal in your stocking once upon a time? Were you a bad little boy?"

He didn't like talking about himself. Liked talking about his past even less. He tried to put all that stuff out of his mind. So it surprised him when he opened his mouth and said, "There were plenty of years I didn't even have a stocking."

She looked as startled as he felt and she straightened in her seat. "That's the most I've ever heard you say about your childhood."

"Don't start feeling sorry for me." He growled. "I hate it when people feel sorry for me."

"Were your parents really poor or—"

"That's all you get," he said and glanced at his watch.

"You're running away."

"I'm not running away," he denied. "I have to head over to the station. See what progress is being made on the arson investigation." He pulled his wallet from his pocket, peeled off a couple of twenties to cover their meal and the tip. Once he scooted across the seat, he got to his feet.

"But you'll keep your promise, right? You won't railroad Clausen into prison just because it's easy."

"I thought your boss took the case away from you." Noah shrugged into his jacket.

"He did, but that doesn't mean I don't care."

"You care too much," he said.

Her chin shot up defiantly. "You don't care enough."

"Is that so?" Noah leaned down, getting in her face.

Alana's hands clutched the Formica tabletop, but she did not draw back or flinch. She gulped. Held her ground. Even though the pale blue vein at her throat fluttered wildly.

He was close enough to kiss her. He sure as hell wanted to kiss her. He would not kiss her. Not here. Not yet.

But somewhere, and soon.

3

ALANA FELT LIKE a treasure seeker who'd just mined a tiny flake of pure gold from a hard, craggy stone. Noah had confirmed what she'd long suspected. He'd had an awful childhood. So bad that he couldn't talk about it. Was that what made him so skittish when it came to intimate relationships?

Um, he wasn't acting skittish just now.

In fact, she was certain he'd been about to kiss her, but in the end, had thought better of it.

She took a sip of her tea, now tepid, and tried to imagine the vulnerable boy he'd once been. It was impossible seeing that masculine jaw as anything but rough, strong and confident. Yet, at one time, he had been a child. He aroused her curiosity.

Oh, who was she kidding? He'd aroused much more than her curiosity.

And the fact that she was off the Clausen case meant that they had nothing to clash about. No conflict of interest standing between them. And she believed him when he said that he would search for exculpatory evidence to prove Clausen's innocence.

Noah had his faults (being emotionally closed off being chief among them) but he was always straightforward and honest. Which was probably why he would never rise much higher than sergeant. He didn't play politics. He was the exact opposite of the strategic men in her family. He operated out of integrity and gut instinct, not cunning tactics.

Ah-hem. There's a reason you didn't hook up with him last summer. But for the life of her, Alana could not remember what that reason was.

METHODICALLY, Noah combed through the burned-out debris of the Price Mansion the morning after his dinner with Alana. Daylight shed a whole new perspective on the scene. He could see things he'd missed in the dark. Bic was still writing up the details of his assessment, but he'd assured Noah that the fire was definitely arson.

Yesterday evening, Noah had dropped by the hospital to check on the Jane Doe victim found unconscious in the mansion's foyer. She'd come out of her coma, but unfortunately, the trauma of the accident had left her with amnesia. The doctor told Noah that while he expected the woman to regain her memory within a few days, she might never be able to recall exactly what had happened the night of the fire.

It was up to Noah and his team to get to the bottom of the blaze. That is, if Clausen hadn't done it. Alana seemed convinced of the man's innocence, but Noah wasn't so easily swayed.

And yet, here he was.

Doing a thorough job. Not for Alana, he told himself, but for justice.

He went back over ground that had already been covered by himself, his team and Bic. Sometimes all it took was a fresh perspective to see things in a different way. Today, Noah claimed that fresh perspective by thinking like an arsonist instead of a cop.

Laypeople often thought that pyromaniacs caused most arsons, but in reality there were very few true pyromaniacs who set fires simply for the sexual thrill they got from watching things burn. It was the motive he'd offered Alana on the night he'd arrested Clausen, but even as he'd said it, he'd known that was the big hole in his case.

Clausen had no history of arson. In fact, he'd never gotten so much as a parking ticket. If Clausen was a true firebug, he would have shown signs of it in his teens or early twenties when pyromania peaked. If Clausen *was* the culprit, there had to be another motive.

Other motives for fire-setting included vandalism, revenge, crime concealment, to terrorize or for profit. Noah ticked through the motives one by one. Vandalism. Could be a gang thing. Except as an upper-middle-class suburb of D.C., Pine Crest experienced almost no gang related crime.

What about revenge? Now there was a possibility.

Noah paced the foyer where he'd found the belt from Clausen's Santa suit. Pausing, he closed his eyes and put his head in the mind of a revenge seeker. Someone had wronged him. He was determined to get even.

Revenge was a dish best served cold. He'd have time to think about it. Be methodical. Make sure an innocent victim like Jane Doe was not in the house before he burned it down. Then again, maybe Jane Doe wasn't so innocent.

Crime concealment? Had the arson been a cover? Had the arsonist meant to kill Jane Doe in the fire? If so, he'd done a poor job of it. If Noah was going to kill someone and use a fire to hide the crime, he'd make damn sure the person was dead before he started the blaze.

Noah opened his eyes, ran a hand over his jaw.

Terrorism? But what was the purpose of a terroristic arson if some terrorist group didn't lay claim to the arson? No one would know that was the reason for the fire, so no one would be terrorized by the act.

That left profit. Good old-fashioned greed. Money. The number-one motivator of criminal behavior.

Who would benefit from burning down the Price Mansion? The city owned the mansion. How could anyone profit from destroying the building that drew so many tourists, and their dollars, to Pine Crest?

"Yoo-hoo, Detective," a woman called, snapping Noah from his concentration.

He looked up to see the scrawny older woman that he'd interviewed the night of the fire. She stood beyond the crime scene tape, waving a hand. Noah dusted his hands against his pants legs and wandered over to where she waited.

"Miss Gaines," he said.

Her narrow face folded into a smile. "You remembered my name."

His boss would have sweet-talked her with a line like "You're very memorable," but Noah cared more about solving crime than the artifice of flattery. "When it comes to the cases I work, I remember everything."

She nodded. "You're a serious young man."

"Is there something I can do for you, Miss Gaines?"

"My memory is not as good as yours, and I just realized something when I saw your car parked over here."

He leaned closer, his interest piqued. "What's that?"

"The same time that I saw Santa leaving the mansion, there was a car parked at the curb right where yours is parked now."

"Did Santa get into the vehicle?"

She shook her head. "No, no. He walked away."

"Which direction?"

"South." She pointed. "He kept walking until he disappeared into the darkness."

"So tell me more about this car."

"It was a sedan. I'm sorry that I don't know the makes of

car models these days. They all look alike, but…" She trailed off, shot him a coy expression.

"But what?"

"You're not going to guess?"

Noah held onto his patience. She was probably lonely and enjoyed milking the suspense. He recalled she'd said she used to be a drama teacher. "It's your stage, Miss Gaines. You've got the spotlight. Tell me what you saw."

"There was a logo on the door." She paused, extracted a tube of rose-scented lotion from the pocket of her jacket and squeezed some into her palms.

Obligatorily, he asked, "What kind of logo?"

She rubbed her hands together. "I think it was a logo of a real estate development company."

"Did you happen to see the name on the logo?"

"Sorry, I didn't."

"Was anyone in the car?"

"I couldn't tell."

This was getting him nowhere. "Thank you, Miss Gaines. I appreciate your efforts. If you do remember more, please give me a call."

"Always happy to help."

He stood there watching her walk away, pondering what she had just told him. The car with the real estate developer logo on it might be nothing. Probably was nothing. But in Noah's mind, the doubt had been raised.

Alana very well might be right. Clausen could be innocent.

And if she was, that left Noah with more questions than answers. One thing was certain. He had a lot more digging to do.

TWO DAYS LATER, "Have Yourself a Merry Little Christmas" was playing on the radio as Alana drove home from work. The DA had called to say exculpatory evidence had come to light in the Clausen case and the charges against him had been dropped. She felt both grateful and vindicated. She'd been right, but more than that, Noah had kept his promise. He'd gone out and found evidence that vindicated her client. Well, not her client, since Dwight had taken the case away from her—but that didn't matter. All that mattered was that an innocent, if slightly nutty, man would go free.

Noah had melted her heart.

Stop it.

Still, she couldn't help smiling. She turned onto Juniper Lane, took the rolling road that ran past the Pine Crest cemetery. She drove this route every day, mostly never even glanced in the direction of the tombstones lined up on the sloping hillside, but today something drew her attention in that direction.

A man in a dark overcoat trudged up the hill toward the cemetery gates, a bouquet of bright red roses in his hand.

The visual was compelling. A lonely figure cast against a dour gray sky, the tall black wrought-iron gates rising up, the bright clutch of flowers the sole contrast to the melancholy scene. The man seemed hauntingly familiar.

She slowed, craned her neck. Who was that?

He lifted his head.

Noah.

Her heart skipped a beat. Noah was going into the cemetery.

Alana couldn't say what compelled her, but she pulled over at the curb and cut the car's engine. She sat there a moment, listening to her heart pounding and staring at the numbers on the dashboard clock.

Don't interrupt the man while he's grieving.

She had no intention of interrupting him, even though she owed him a big "thank you." She should drive away.

But curiosity had her easing open the car door and she got out, shutting it quietly behind her. She breathed in a breath of bracingly cold winter air and started toward the cemetery gates, hands stuffed deeply into the pockets of her wool camel coat.

What are you doing?

She ambled down the rows, the wind burning the tops of her ears. She hunched her shoulders against the cold. The massive cemetery was pre–Civil War and it was filled with tall, thick trees and family mausoleums. He moved in and out of her line of vision, hidden at times by trees or tombs.

This is stupid. Go back to your car.

Noah was several yards ahead of her. What was she going to do? Pretend to be visiting a grave? Why was she following him?

She slowed, almost turned back, but a pressing need to know more about him pushed her forward. Her pulse quickened. What was she afraid of?

When she reached the row Noah had turned down, a handy excuse on her lips for why she'd bumped into him in the cemetery, she was surprised to find no one there. Had she turned down the wrong row?

She wandered along, trepidation building. Had Noah been married before? Was he a widower? She hadn't heard any rumors of that nature, but he was a secretive man.

Then she spied it.

The bouquet of roses, fresh and fragile, propped against the cold slate headstone. She minced closer, left the narrow cement walkway, the heels of her shoes sinking into the damp earth. She stood swaying in the wind, reading the headstone.

Helen Jayne Briscoe
November 1, 1962 to December 25 1992
Beloved mother of Noah

Alana blinked as the truth hit her. Noah's mother had died on Christmas Day when he was around ten or eleven years old. Immediately empathy seized her. Emotion clogged her throat. Poor kid. Poor guy. No wonder he hated Christmas.

She tried to imagine what that was like, but she had no idea. She'd never lost anyone close to her. She was blessed and she knew it. How could she hope to relate to Noah and what he'd suffered?

Alana straightened, glanced around for Noah, but he was gone.

Resolve rose inside her, sharp and urgent. Dammit, she was not going to let him be alone this Christmas. Not on the twentieth anniversary of his mother's death.

Whether Noah wanted it or not, she was determined to bring the spirit of Christmas into his life. He might not be able to admit it, but he needed her.

NOAH STEPPED OUT of the shower. Toweled himself dry. Turned an irritating question over in his head.

Why had Alana been trailing him through the cemetery?

He'd known she was behind him. He was a cop after all, and she was not particularly adept at surveillance. Then again, she was a lawyer. Why would she be? Her skills lay in other areas. So he'd quickly left the flowers on his mother's grave and slipped out the side gate. Hurried to his SUV.

Another question. Why had he left the flowers behind when he knew Alana would find them and put two and two together?

Every answer he could think of was a rationalization except the one he wished he could deny. He'd *wanted* her to know what he could not bring himself to tell her face-to-face. And that bothered him most of all.

The doorbell rang.

Deftly, he cinched the towel at his waist, padded to the front door. He put an eye to the peephole. There, on his front stoop, stood Alana holding a cardboard box and wearing a headband with reindeer antlers affixed to it.

Seriously?

Don't answer the door. Right. Except his car was parked right out front. She knew he was home. He cursed under his breath.

The doorbell rang again.

He could take another tack. Go on the offensive. Chase her off. Open the door wearing nothing but a towel and see how long it took her to turn tail and run. He was guessing less than ten seconds.

Cocking a devilish grin, he yanked the door open, his fingers still pinching the towel closed around his waist.

At the same time he opened the door, she raised her fist, preparing to knock. Momentum had hold of her and she ended up rapping her knuckles against his chest.

He jumped back.

So did she.

Her eyes widened, but Alana was smooth and sophisticated and she quickly schooled her expression. "Oh," she said. "Were you in the shower?"

He bit back a smart retort and instead stabbed his free hand through his wet hair, sending droplets of water spattering around him.

She hesitated.

He counted off the seconds. Three…two…one.

But instead of leaving, she squared her shoulders, tossed her head back and sailed past him into his apartment. His mistake, standing so that there was space between his body and the door.

He followed her, shutting the door behind him. His gaze licked over her rocking-hot body. She wore a short red plaid-wool skirt that showed off dynamite legs encased in black tights, giving her a sexy grown-up schoolgirl look. Snowmen earrings danced at her earlobes whenever she moved her head.

"What are you doing here?" he asked.

"Spreading Christmas cheer." She beamed, depositing her box on his coffee table.

"Excuse me?"

You asked for this. You left the flowers on your mother's grave instead of confronting her in the cemetery. Now she thinks she's on a mission to make the Grinch feel loved.

"No wonder you're such a grump at Christmas. No decorations. Nothing to cheer you up." She waved a hand at his apartment decorated in what could best be described as bare essentials. Couch, coffee table, lamp, TV. All of the characterless variety.

Once he'd been absorbed into the foster care system, he'd grown up without having anything that was truly his own. That lack of attachment might make some people crave individuality or develop an excessive need to possess things But for Noah, it meant he really didn't give a damn about ownership. The more you had, the more there was to lose.

Alana's gaze grazed over him and her cheeks were bright pink, but she was undeterred by his near nakedness. He stepped closer.

She backed up. Her muscles tensed. Her lips quivered the tiniest bit. Her breathing quickened, her chest rising and falling underneath that red-and-green sweater that hugged her breasts.

Ah, she wasn't as self-possessed as she wanted him to believe. But hell, neither was he. His mouth was dry and his—

Damn it!

"I'm gonna go put on some clothes," he mumbled, surprised to hear his voice come out thick and raspy.

"Good idea." She nodded.

As he hurried to the safety of his bedroom, it occurred to Noah that he'd been the one to turn tail and run.

4

WHAT WAS SHE doing here?

Alana swallowed, raised a hand to her mouth as Noah disappeared down the hallway. She couldn't resist watching him walk away. She sighed. What a beautiful butt.

Yes, but don't get caught up in the physical. You're here to chisel through his wall. Let him know he's not alone. Let him know you care. Show him that Christmas is, indeed, special.

Right.

She blew out her breath through puffed cheeks, the vision of Noah's butt barely cloaked by that thin cotton towel burned into her brain.

Focus.

Resolutely, she turned to the box she'd brought with her and started taking out decorations, including a small artificial tree. Multi-colored indoor twinkle lights. Scented holiday candles (cinnamon, gingerbread and pine.) An eight-inch Santa figurine that lit up. Red-and-white striped candy canes. Artificial snow in an aerosol can. A cluster of fresh mistletoe she'd clipped from the tree in her backyard and tied with a festive red ribbon.

She set the tree up. She'd wanted to bring a big tree, complete with lights, but baby steps. This would be invasion enough for a dyed-in-the-wool holiday hater. In fact, she half expected him to toss her out on her ear.

"Okay, O'Hara," Noah said.

Alana jumped, spun around. She hadn't heard him come back into the room. Her pulse raced. The man could seriously have a career as a cat burglar.

He wore khaki pants and a black turtleneck sweater. On some men a turtleneck looked dorky, but on Noah the garment further served to illustrate the cat burglar image—stealthy, secretive, intriguing. Alana flicked out her tongue to moisten her lips.

"What's this?" He gestured toward the Christmas ornaments she'd strewn over his couch as she'd started sorting them out.

"I wanted to thank you for going the extra mile on the Clausen case. The DA told me that you'd found evidence that cleared him."

"The arson investigator was able to narrow down the time the blaze was set to a thirty-minute window. Clausen was caught on the surveillance camera at a twenty-four-hour grocery store on the other side of town during that time frame."

"I'm happy for him," she said. "And I appreciate what you did."

Noah sauntered toward her, coming closer and closer until he was within touching distance. Alana gulped, but stood her ground. She'd been around enough cops to know that invading someone's personal space was a show of dominance. Well, she wasn't about to be dominated.

"Is that all this is about? Gratitude?"

She nodded, unable to find her voice.

"No attempt at all to make me feel all warm and fuzzy about Christmas?"

"Everyone should feel warm and fuzzy about Christmas," she said.

"No trying to turn Scrooge into a nice man?"

"Who, me?"

"In spite of being an attorney, you haven't really learned a lot of the dark side of life, huh, O'Hara?"

Alana raised her chin. "Only since I've known you, Briscoe."

"Touché." A wry smile tipped his lips as he took another step toward her.

Her gaze latched onto his. She refused to look away, but the heat! It was like a sauna in here. Sweat pooled between her breasts, slid down the back of her neck.

"I could just throw you and your Merry Christmas attitude out of my apartment."

"You could, but then you'd drown in bitterness and bah humbug."

"And what's so bad about that?"

"You're too young to be the grumpy old man who yells at kids for cutting across your lawn."

"I don't have a lawn."

"Metaphorically speaking."

"So." He canted his head, drilled his stare straight into her. It was all she could do not to blink. "You're here to save me from myself."

"I'm here to save you from Scrooge's vision of Christmas Future."

"Aren't you considerate."

"Sarcasm is a symptom, not an antidote."

"What does that mean?" He cocked an eyebrow, sent her a sardonic smile.

"It's okay to have fun."

"With all the ills in the world?"

"Because of all the ills in the world. I'm here to shine a little light."

"Aren't I the lucky one?" One sardonic eyebrow went up on his forehead.

"Yes, lucky that I care." The minute the words were out of her mouth, Alana wished she could snatch them back.

"You care about me, huh?" His voice lowered.

She shrugged. "Well, you know, as a person."

"That's it?" He took another step. If she didn't back up, soon he was going to be standing on top of her.

She gulped. "I care about a lot of people."

"And yet…" His voice dropped, lower, deeper. "Here you are, decorating *my* place."

"You're the only one I know who hasn't decorated."

"You're not a very good liar," he observed. "Must make being a defense attorney quite a chore."

"Who says I'm lying?"

"You've got a tell."

She could feel the warmth of his breath against her cheek. He smelled like spearmint. "A tell?"

"The tops of your ears turn pink when you lie. FYI. When you're lying, cover your ears."

She reached up. The reindeer antler headband pulled her hair back from her ears, exposing everything. She yanked off the headband, tossed it over her shoulder. Tousled her hair to camouflage her ears. "Sayonara, human lie detector."

Another step closer and there he was. The toes of his shoes butted up against hers. Her pulse sprinted, bounding against her wrist.

"What are you doing?" she asked.

"Spreading some holiday cheer." He echoed what she'd told him when she'd arrived. He bent down, brushing her shoulder in the process, and retrieved the cluster of mistletoe.

An instant tingle shot down her nerve endings and her chest tightened.

Reaching up, Noah looped the mistletoe's red ribbon

around the overhead lamp. Now they were standing directly under it.

He snaked one arm around her waist, his grip strong and certain.

"Oh," Alana exclaimed, her head spinning with the swiftness of it all. The heat was back, more blistering than ever, and her knees, well, they were wimps. Giving out on her.

His eyes sparkled in the light. A long, tense moment passed between them. Alana couldn't move. Didn't want to move. It felt so good here in his arms.

"You really came over here for this," he said, his tone matter-of-fact. "Didn't you?"

She put both hands up to cover her ears. "No."

He smiled. Wickedly. "You really should become a prosecutor. Lying doesn't suit you. Or maybe you're just in denial."

"Of what?" She was starting to get irritated.

He dipped his head. She leaned back against his arm. Their lips were almost touching. A second passed. Then two. Then three. "Your feelings."

"For you?" She tried a derisive hoot, but it came out as shaky as her legs. "You're the one in denial, Briscoe."

"I wasn't the one who pulled the plug on us. Remember?"

Yes, she'd been the one to pull the plug on their budding relationship when he wouldn't open up to her. Refused to talk about his feelings. He'd been Mister-Keep-Things-Light, when she'd known he possessed the power to burn down her life if she let him get too close. So why was she here?

"Tell me that I don't haunt your dreams the way you haunt mine," he murmured.

He dreamed of her? She couldn't move. Couldn't breathe. Couldn't think. Her pulse, which had been skipping red-hot through her veins, iced up.

"No," she whispered.

His fingertips brushed back her hair, revealing an ear. "Ah." He chuckled. "Ah-hah."

Noah tightened his grip on her waist and Alana gulped against the surge of sexual electricity snapping between them. His other hand eased to the nape of her neck, fingers plowing through her hair, his mouth seeking hers in exquisite slow motion.

He was going to kiss her and, damn her, Alana was going to let him.

His mouth closed over hers and...*bliss!*

She'd missed his kiss much more than she'd realized. Everywhere he touched her, sparks flew. Her skin sizzled. Her stomach hummed. Her muscles twitched.

He made a triumphant noise in the back of his throat and deepened the kiss, darting his tongue past her teeth, exploring her fully. His invasion sent desire spiraling through her.

A sweet sound of need, that she had not meant to express, slipped from her lips. She grabbed his shoulders between her hands, intent on pushing him away, but instead she pulled him closer. Egged him on.

He stole her breath, robbed her reason, made it impossible to think of anything but him.

Finally, when her head was mush and her legs were jelly, he slowly moved his lips from hers. "Alana." He breathed. "You haunt me."

Her brain fought through the hormone-induced fog, struggling to make sense of what had just happened. She'd allowed him to kiss her again. Rekindled something she believed they'd put to rest.

He dropped his arms and she felt suddenly *naked* without the protection of his embrace. He stepped away, turned his back to her. Moved to the window. Parted the blinds. Stared out.

Withdrawing.

Just like he always did when things got too intense between them. The man sent mixed messages and she refused to be his yo-yo.

Why not? There's nothing wrong with being a yo-yo. It's a fun toy.

Toy. Precisely. She cared about Noah too much to simply be his plaything.

But he was the picture of loneliness, standing at the window, the winter sunlight bathing him in silhouette. Looking at him hurt her heart. He put up a tough front, but she saw the chinks in his armor. Resolutely, she pasted on a smile, started humming "Jingle Bell Rock" and went back to her decorating as if nothing had happened.

NOAH STUDIED THE people on the sidewalk below. Couples holding hands. Shoppers bustling by with brightly colored packages. Parents corralling kids. He balled his hands into fists, his mind scrambling with a mosaic of longing, lust and recrimination.

He hadn't spoken another word to Alana since he'd kissed her. He'd assume she would just leave. But she hadn't left. She was moving around behind him, singing Christmas songs. His lips still tingled from the kiss. His arousal still stiff. He wanted to say something, but he couldn't think of what to say. Why hadn't she left or at least said something?

What the hell had he thought he was doing? Why had he kissed her? They'd already been down this road, and decided it was a dead end. He'd lost control and losing control disturbed him.

He had to see her on a regular basis. He had to learn how to deal with this attraction without acting on it. Yes, she'd come to his place, but he should have been able to rein in his impulses. The fact that he hadn't been able to do so ate at him.

Her scent was all around him. She smelled of oranges,

nutmeg and hope. Damn that hope. Her taste lingered in his mouth—fresh and clean and womanly. He narrowed his eyes at the passersby, willed himself to think of something else, anything else besides Alana.

But how could he blot her out when she was jingling bells and lighting cinnamon candles and filling his apartment with her sweet voice. He had nothing to offer her. Couldn't she see that? Didn't she understand he'd lost his ability to completely trust others? Wasn't that what he'd really been hoping she would learn when he left the flowers on his mother's grave where he knew she would see them? He didn't want her sympathy. Rather, he'd wanted her understanding.

So just tell her that.

Noah shook his head. He didn't know how.

Finally, he turned, preparing an excuse for why he had to leave. Why she had to leave. He opened his mouth, but no words came out. In just a few short minutes, she'd transformed his dour living room into a welcoming holiday tableau.

A miniature Christmas tree sat in the corner. Mary, Joseph and the whole nativity crew adorned his coffee table. A Santa figurine waved at him from beside the tree. Candles flickered. Colored lights twinkled gaily.

"Well," she said, hands clasped behind her back. "What do you think?"

Noah made a tactical error. He met her eager gaze.

Brilliant blue eyes widened, taking him in. Pink lips, still swollen from his kiss, parted into a sweet circle. Her hair was sexily mussed. Her sweater revealed a tantalizing glimpse of cleavage. One slim hand rested on her hip, her back arched slightly. The gesture caused the hem of her skirt to rise up, showing off even more of those long, lean legs.

"I think…"

"Yes?" Her face brightened. She straightened.

Ah, hell. He wanted to tell her everything. About his mother's death. About his experiences in the foster care system, but he just couldn't do it. He did what he always did when things turned dicey. He took action.

Noah took two strides to reach her and went in for another kiss.

She met him halfway, tipping up her chin, opening her mouth, her tongue touching his, her arms going around his neck, pulling his head down to hers. Noah's arms folded around her narrow waist and he tugged her flush against his chest once more, those luscious breasts pressed against his hard muscles.

Her hot little mouth burned him from the outside in. Her taut thighs flexed. The feel of her supple body turned his erection stone-hard. He kissed her lips and then moved down to nibble her chin. She let out a soft, desperate moan.

"Noah," she gasped, her fingers threading through his hair.

He drew back and peered into blue eyes as enticing as sapphires. "Yes," he murmured.

"I can't… This isn't…" She paused.

He held his breath.

She shook her head. Put on the brakes. "I shouldn't have come here."

"I know," he said gruffly. "I know."

"I don't want to lead you on."

"Same here."

"Our jobs—"

"Gotcha. Opposite sides of the fence."

"It's not you. You're a great guy."

"You don't have to make up an excuse. I get it."

"It's not that I don't want to, because I do. I do."

Noah held up a palm, trying hard to hold onto some dignity, fighting off the caveman inside him that just wanted to scoop her up and take her to bed and let the consequences be damned. "We've been through this before. It's why we broke up before."

"We didn't break up. We were never together."

"It's why we were never together. You're Merry Christmas. I'm Bah Humbug. You look for the best in people. I go right for the skeletons in the closet. You're light. I'm dark—"

"You're scared to death of intimacy and I'm not," she finished for him.

"Right. There you go. Polar opposites."

"Opposites attract."

"On the surface, maybe, but not for good. Not for the long haul."

"Why did you kiss me? Just so you could break up with me?"

"I'm not breaking up with you. We were never together. You said so yourself." Noah took a step back.

"You're making me crazy, you know that? Before I met you, I was a perfectly sane person. Now I'm doing dumb things like stalking you in cemeteries and decorating your place for Christmas when clearly you don't want it decorated."

Her cheeks were flushed, her eyes filled with distress. He'd caused that distress. Why was he treating her like this? She didn't deserve to be strung along, but the thought of losing all hope with her tore him up inside.

Hells bells, what do you want, Briscoe?

"It's my problem. I know it. I have this need to help people. It's why I'm a defense attorney instead of a prosecutor." Her hands fluttered about her face. "Clearly, you don't want my help, but I keep pushing like you're going to change your mind if I just keep pushing, and you're not going to change your mind—"

Noah took hold of her and kissed her again. He'd made her feel terrible for being open and honest and giving. That had never been his intention. He'd wanted to chase her off because he was no good for her, but she couldn't seem to see that.

She kissed him with a ferocity that took his breath, and then when she was done, she pushed back against his chest. "We've got chemistry. Of that there is no doubt. I like you, Noah. I'd like to explore this thing between us, but you're not ready for a serious relationship. I am. It's what I want. So, I'm breaking things off with you again before we do something that we both live to regret."

Noah wanted to tell her that he was ready for a serious relationship, but he couldn't force the words from his throat. He worried that if he declared his desires out loud something terrible would immediately befall him. Other than his job, whenever he'd gotten close to getting something he wanted, it turned to dust in his hands. He feared that if he laid his heart on the line, that Alana would crush it under her sexy little heels. They were opposites, after all.

Coward. You're just making excuses because you're afraid to take a chance.

Hell, yes, he was afraid. He'd never allowed anyone to get too close. It's why all his previous affairs had ended.

This one was ending before it ever began. As he got older he was generating less traction in relationships, not more, as most people did.

Gotta change, Briscoe, if you ever want things to be different.

"Merry Christmas, Noah," Alana said. "You can keep the decorations. I have plenty." With a sad smile, she kissed his cheek. Picked up her empty cardboard box. Walked away.

And he just let her go.

Leaving him with a plethora of holiday cheer, the lingering aroma of her citrusy scent and a hard, tight knot in his stomach.

5

ALANA HAD ONE goal for the holiday season. Stay out of Noah Briscoe's line of fire. Which wasn't that easy to do, since her job brought her to the police station on a daily basis. Unfortunately, the man was a workaholic and he always seemed to be there.

It was childish, but whenever she saw him, she pretended to be engrossed in something—her smartphone, a chip in her nail polish, a legal brief. He let it slide, walking past her, glancing at his watch, looking relieved that she was pretending not to see him. But every time she turned her head and his surreptitious gaze met hers, goose bumps spread up her arms.

Dammit! The man carried too much emotional baggage. Why was she so interested in him?

Why? Because beneath that tough exterior lurked the heart of a wounded man just aching to be loved. She could see it in his eyes, but he was too proud to let her in.

Fine. Great. It wasn't her job to save him from himself.

Anyway, some people just couldn't be saved.

But Noah was not a lost cause. He did care. He coached basketball at the Pine Crest youth center in his spare time. He gave blood every two months. She knew because she did, too. He was incredibly gentle with the children of parents he'd had to lock up. He—

Rationalizations, Alana. You're grasping for reasons not to run away. For your own mental health, you've got to stop this.

Right.

Especially since she was attending her firm's annual Christmas party with a date, and all she could do was wish it was Noah's palm pressed against the small of her back.

Gunter Smith was tall, blond and gorgeous in a Nordic way. They'd gone to school together at Georgetown. Currently, he was a defense attorney practicing law in D.C. but he was considering a move to Pine Crest. He was ready, he'd told her when he called to let her know he'd been invited to the party, to settle down, get married, have kids. He should have been perfect for her. He ticked all the right boxes. Great genes. Toothy smile. No darkness in his past.

And Gunter bored her out of her skull.

Alana wore a black cocktail dress. The hem was a little too high. She'd bought it with Noah in mind. Now, Gunter was the one eyeing her legs with a lascivious look in his eyes. His tailored suit, tight muscles and stylish haircut should have turned her on. They did not. He was too slick, too pretty, too damn smug when he talked about how much money he made freeing wealthy, but oh-so-guilty, criminals. He actually laughed about it.

"I love the law," Gunter said. "It's such a cat and mouse game."

"But you do care about justice, right?"

"Justice is in the eye of the beholder." He winked. "For instance, you do that dress justice."

Alana, who'd been holding onto a glass of wine for the past half-hour, swallowed the whole thing down. It was going to be a long night.

Gunter's eyes glistened. "Shall I get you another?"

"Yes, please," she said, more for a little distance than a real desire for wine.

"Be right back." He smiled and disappeared in the crowd.

She blew out her breath and wondered what Noah was doing on this Saturday night the weekend before Christmas.

"Alana," Dwight Jacoby called her name as he strode toward her looking purposeful.

"What's up?"

"I just got a call from the police station. The cops made another high-profile arrest in the Price Mansion arson. I know you were miffed at me for pulling you off the case when Clausen stirred media attention. To make amends, if this case goes to trial, I want you as second chair."

"Seriously?"

He nodded. "You deserve it."

"Who did they arrest?"

"Teague Price."

"The real estate developer?"

"And great nephew to Colin T. Price."

Two emotions struck her at once—exuberance over being invited to serve as second chair, the number-one support position to the primary trial lawyer—and trepidation over having to knock heads with Noah again.

Gunter returned, handed her a glass of wine and slipped an arm around her waist. When he splayed his fingers over her butt, it decided the issue. She'd much rather be at the police station with Noah than stranded at this party with a grabby defense attorney looking to score.

"I'm so sorry, Gunter," she said, stepping away from him. "A client has just been arrested. Dwight and I have to go interview him."

"Now? Tonight?" Gunter looked disappointed.

"I'm afraid so." She turned to her boss. "I'm ready."

"You're going to the police station dressed like that?" A disapproving frown creased Gunter's brow.

Alana tossed her head. "Yes," she said. "Yes, I am."

"I'll call you later," Gunter said. "Give you a chance to make things up to me for skipping out on our date."

"No." Alana pushed the wine glass into his hand. "I don't think that's such a good idea."

"But…but…" Gunter stammered. "On paper we'd be so good together."

"Paper isn't life, Gunter," she said. "Sometimes the best person for you looks terrible on a pros and cons list."

"I don't get you."

"My point exactly," she said.

WHEN ALANA WALKED into the interrogation room with Dwight, Noah's jaw dropped.

For one thing, he hadn't expected to see her here. Not with the way she'd been avoiding him. Not when Jacoby had taken the Clausen case away from her. For another thing, he had not expected to see her wearing a hot little black dress that showed a generous expanse of firm, trim thigh and a pair of heartbreaker stilettos. The way she looked gliding into the interrogation room, demure pearls strung around her neck, started the mental reel on his X-rated fantasies.

He ached to reach across the desk to touch her. To say something personal, intimate. Compliment her beauty, beg her to forgive him for being such a stupid fool, but of course he could not do that.

Jacoby took a seat beside his client, Teague Price. Alana sat beside Jacoby, directly across from Noah. His eyes met hers. She didn't shy, didn't avoid his gaze, but try as he might, he could not decipher what she was thinking.

Once the lawyers were ready, Noah began the interrogation. Based on the tip he'd gotten from Agnes Gaines about the car parked outside the Price Mansion on the night of the fire, he'd had his team comb the street for evidence. The debris they'd collected from curbside had taken the lab techs several days to sift through, but eventually they'd found a candy bar wrapper with Teague Price's fingerprints on it.

Noah had done more digging and discovered Teague had been in some trouble as a young man for starting fires. Plus, Teague was disgruntled when the rest of the Price family had voted to turn the mansion over to the city for upkeep as a historical landmark. He'd wanted the mansion torn down in order to build an exclusive country club on the lot because it was adjacent to the golf course he already had in development. The Price family still owned the land itself. With the mansion gone, nothing stood in the way of Teague's goal. That took care of motive.

Now for opportunity.

Noah stated the exact date for the record, then asked, "Where were you the night the Price Mansion burned?"

Teague shoved a hand through his silver hair. "I was home watching television."

"Alone?"

He shrugged. "My wife was at her bridge club meeting."

Ah, so no alibi.

Noah continued the questioning, but he couldn't fully concentrate. He kept smelling Alana's cologne, feeling the heat of her gaze on her face, and listening to the sound of her soft breathing as a soothing sound track to Teague's denials.

Snap out of it, Briscoe. Don't let her mess with your head.

After half an hour, he finished up his questions. For the time being he had to let Teague go free, but his gut told him the man was guilty and he wasn't going to stop until he found enough evidence to charge him with a crime.

"One last thing, Mr. Price," Noah said when everyone in the room was on their feet. "We'd like to search your house.

Since you have nothing to hide, I'm sure you won't mind if we just have a short walk through."

"Get a warrant," Jacoby said, hustling his client toward the door.

The lawyer knew as well as Noah that they didn't have enough evidence yet to convince a judge to issue a search warrant.

Alana lingered behind Jacoby and Price. Her gaze caressed his.

He wanted to say something, to tell her how her decorating his apartment had cheered him up, to ask her if she'd give him another chance. But this wasn't the time or place for such entreaties.

"Alana," Jacoby called.

"I have to go," she whispered to Noah.

"I know."

She raised a hand, looked wistful.

He stood watching her go, his stare fixed on that short skirt as she sashayed away.

Mind whirling with the conflicting agendas of pursuing Alana and digging up more dirt on Teague Price, Noah stopped by his office. He logged off his computer, shrugged into his winter coat, and headed out to the parking lot.

It was almost midnight. Christmas lights glowed from the surrounding buildings. Noah tugged in a breath of frosty air, heard the clicking of a car's unresponsive starter. He turned his head in the direction of the noise.

The noise came from a silver late-model compact car. Alana's car.

Immediately, he was at her car door.

She rolled down the window, looking sheepish. "I forgot to renew my roadside assistance membership."

"No worries," he said. "I'll give you a ride."

"I probably just need a jump."

He couldn't help grinning, although capitalizing on sexual innuendo wasn't his style. "It's not the battery," he said. "It's the starter."

"How can you tell?"

"Your headlights are on. If it was the battery, your headlights wouldn't come on."

"Oh."

He patted the roof of the car. "Come on. I'll take you home."

ALANA SAT IN THE passenger seat of Noah's SUV, fully aware of how high her skirt crept up when she sat down.

Noah cut a glance over at her legs, a smile hung on his lips. He noticed, too. "Nice dress."

Her pulse did something weird and her cheeks flushed hot. She yanked on the hem, futilely trying to tug it lower.

He started the engine, but kept his eyes trained on her. Tension tightened her muscles. "Where do you live?"

It surprised her to realize that although they'd been flirting and dancing around this on again/off again relationship for months, he'd never been to her house. She gave him directions.

They drove in silence, but the quiet was too much for her to bear. "You really think Teague Price is the arsonist."

"I do." He recited the reasons he suspected the real estate developer, right down to his past history for arson.

"I agree," she said.

"You do?" he sounded surprised.

"Jacoby's making me his second chair on this case."

"Hey, that's big."

"Assuming it goes to trial of course. You don't have nearly enough evidence to convict."

"I'll get it."

Alana canted her head. "I believe you."

"We probably shouldn't be talking about this," he said. "Since we're on opposite sides."

"It seems like we're always on opposite sides."

"Too bad you don't work for the prosecution."

"Too bad," she echoed and was startled to find that she meant it.

Five minutes later, he pulled to a stop outside Alana's house.

"You own your own home?" he said.

"I do."

"Home ownership is a big commitment."

"I'm not afraid of commitment."

That killed the conversation. Alana opened the door. "Well, thanks for the ride."

"Hang on, you're not walking up to a dark house by yourself."

"It's not dark." She waved a hand at the lighted Christmas decorations adorning her yard.

"I'm walking you to the door." His tone brooked no argument. He was out of the driver's seat and around to her side before she could put up any further protest.

The truth was he made her feel safe and secure. She *wanted* him to walk her to the door, but she didn't want to feel that way. It was too risky.

He took her arm. She'd left home this evening with one man and was returning on the arm of another. But she was happier now than she'd been then. Much happier with Noah than Gunter.

Noah's touch immediately stirred something inside. They made their way up the sidewalk, past a lighted toy train, faux packages, and a red-nosed reindeer. They passed under the candy-cane archway leading to her front porch. Santa waved from the roof as blue icicle lights blinked off and on.

Okay, maybe she did tend to go overboard at Christmas, but she loved this time of year.

They stopped at her door.

Noah dropped her hand.

She should have mumbled good-night, darted inside, but instead…oh dammit…instead of doing that, she met his gaze.

His eyes were the color of obsidian, dark and unfathomable, his jaw beard-stubbled. His shaggy hair was mussed. He needed a haircut. But even so, he looked devilishly sexy. She couldn't help comparing this strong, rugged man to pretty boy Gunter. There was no comparison. She'd take broody and tortured over perfect any day. Noah had depth and breadth that Gunter could never have. For better or worse, his hard life had formed him, shellacked a hard shell over a tender heart.

And, damn her, she wanted nothing more than to hammer through that shell, expose the vulnerable man beneath the gruff exterior.

Noah propped one arm against the doorframe just above her head and for a second, they just stood there, silhouetted by the lights of the buoyant Christmas ornaments. His gaze hung on her mouth.

Alana's heart throbbed.

Noah made a rough sound low in his throat and lowered his head, angular lips parting as his arms went around her. Helplessly, Alana dropped her purse and lifted her arms, wrapping them around Noah's neck.

His mouth burned hers with a sensual heat. His erection pressed against her thigh, hard and urgent. Alana's body responded, softening in all the right places. He ran a palm over her hair, murmured her name in a raspy bass that sent quivers of desire straight through her.

Her knees could scarcely hold her up. She'd wanted him for months. Dreamed of finishing what they'd started that night in the back seat of his SUV.

"Noah," she gasped, her mind reeling. She thought of all the reasons this was a very bad idea, but her body didn't care. Need burned inside her, hot and insistent.

"Alana." He breathed.

She fumbled for her purse, scooped it up. Searched inside for her house key. Her fingers trembled as she struggled to stab the key into the lock. She could feel Noah standing behind her, wondered what he was thinking.

The door swung inward. She stepped over the threshold. Turned back to him.

He swayed on her step, looking uncertain.

Then Alana reached out, slapped her hand on his chest, wadded his shirt in her fist and pulled him into the house with her.

6

AT THIS POINT, Noah wasn't even thinking. He was pure reaction. He kicked the door closed behind him. Locked it. Bending, he scooped Alana off her feet. She was a feather in his arms.

"Ooo!" she exclaimed.

"Where's your bedroom?" he growled.

"End of the hall," she said, her voice high and breathless.

His shoes echoed against her hardwood floors. His heart thumped. His blood pumped. The door to her bedroom was slightly ajar. He nudged it wider with his knee. Inside a Santa Claus nightlight lit the way.

He carefully lowered her to her feet.

"Alana," he spoke her name again, unable to wrap his head around the fact that he was here in her bedroom at last. He'd been dreaming of this for months.

"Stop talking," she said, "and kiss me."

How could a man argue with that? He'd spent so many years keeping his emotions on a chain that they just boiled over, refusing to be contained one second longer.

He kissed her like he'd never kissed anyone. Long and hard and with all the feelings he'd been denying. Letting his actions say what words could not. *I want you. I need you. I've got to have you, no matter what the consequences.* His hands moved to her breasts, too abrupt, yes, but he itched to touch the soft mounds beneath the silky black dress.

Her delicate hands slipped underneath his jacket, slid up across his back, burning hot trails of sensation through his cotton shirt, searing his skin.

He paused to wrench off his jacket, toss it aside. The room smelled of Christmas cookies, fresh baked and delicious. He pulled her close again, kneed her legs apart. Her dress rose up as she straddled his thigh, the fabric of his slacks rubbing against her bare legs. A sweet gasp of pleasure escaped her lips.

She worked the buttons of his shirt and Noah surrendered any last shred of resistance—letting go of his need to control, yielding to temptation, allowing his libido full rein.

They tore at each other's clothing as if frantically unwrapping Christmas presents, desperate to see what lay inside the pretty packages. She yanked at his shirt. Buttons popped. His fingers found the zipper of her dress and whisked it down. In a flurry of activity, they stripped each other naked.

Panting, they stood looking at each other in the glow of the Santa Claus nightlight, their chests heaving in simultaneous breaths. Looking at her, left Noah both shaky and bold, pushing him over the edge into dangerous territory.

In that moment, he could have backed out. Should have backed out, but she didn't give him a chance to reconsider. Her hands were all over him—her mouth, too. Noah was lost in a sea of kisses, heat and giving feminine flesh.

She clung to his shoulders, her fingernails sinking into his skin. He kissed her lips, her chin and the hollow of her throat. She tasted of salt and woman. She arched her back, pressed urgently against him. Igniting a blaze deep inside Noah.

His reaction throbbed, begging for release. He'd better slow things down or he wouldn't last five minutes. He untangled her arms from his neck, rolled her over on her back and settled her into the down comforter. He gazed down at her, stunned by her beauty. Her glorious auburn hair spread out across plump pillows.

Lowering his head, Noah pressed his lips to her bare belly and then kissed his way back up to her nipples. She quivered beneath his lips. "Do you like that?"

"Mmm," she said in a sultry whisper and laced her fingers through his hair.

He flicked his tongue over one straining nipple and gently nibbled. Her exquisite sound of enjoyment sent reedy blades of pleasure slicing through his solar plexus. When she reached up to strum the pads of her thumbs over his nipples, she had him doing a little moaning of his own.

"Do you like that?" she whispered.

"No," he said.

"What?" She paused, looking alarmed.

"I love it."

She grinned and went back to what she was doing with her mouth, tongue and fingers. After a long, leisurely exploration that left him hauling in shallow gasps of air, she left his nipples and her hand traveled downward. She stroked his abs, traced her fingertips over his taut muscles. The tickling sensation produced crazy, erotic ripples in his belly that undulated all the way down to his groin.

When her fingers grazed his straining erection, she stopped just short of touching his throbbing tip. Her breath was hot against his flesh, inflaming him. Completely undone, Noah groaned.

He stroked and caressed and kissed her until he'd worked them both into a fevered pitch. He couldn't stand one more second not being joined with her.

Alana arched her hips upward, issuing an invitation he could not deny.

"Hang on, sweetheart," he said, leaping off the bed for his pants and grabbing the condom in his wallet. Spurred by pure male instinct, he rushed back to the bed, ripping open the wrapper with his teeth.

"Let me help." She took the condom from him. Rolled it on his rock-hard shaft. Then she dropped open her legs, welcoming him to her.

Noah sank into her delicious heat, stunned by how good she felt. How good they felt linked together. They moved as one, knocking pillows to the floor, thumping the headboard against the wall, squeaking the bedsprings with energetic force.

He struggled to hold onto his release, determined she would go first and when she cried out his name and shuddered in his arms, his need crested, crashed. He followed right behind her, his breathing ragged and rough.

They collapsed against the pillows. Alana held her arm against her waist, her chest rising and falling in jagged jerks. Noah's entire body tingled. He reached over, pulled her to him, held her tight.

He had so many things to say to her. So many things, in fact, that his mind clogged and words evaded him. Nothing he could say seemed adequate to match what he was feeling. He loved being with her. This was great. Better than great. No regrets. No guilt. But damn, he hadn't meant for this to happen.

What did it mean? Where did they go from here?

Ah, hell. He gulped, cradled her against his chest and then slowly told her about his childhood. About the night his mother had died saving him from the house fire. About his life in foster homes.

She never said a word, just let him talk. She hugged him tight and he held her until her eyelids drooped and closed, and her breathing slowed to a steady rhythm. Her head was just below his nose and he could smell the sweet fragrance of her perfume. He kept holding her long after she went to sleep.

Tomorrow there would be expectations. He'd have to deal with the consequences of tonight. But for now, he was in no rush for morning.

He lay there long into the night, enjoying the pressure of her head on his chest, knowing it felt too good to be true. It would be so easy to close his eyes and fall asleep in her bed.

Too damn easy. Spending the night would a send a message that he wasn't sure he wanted to send. What was he supposed to do?

Finally, Noah eased out from under her. He stood there a moment, with the gray pre-dawn light oozing through the sheer curtains, watching her sleep. He wanted to crawl back in bed beside her and hold her for a hundred years, but something wouldn't let him.

Instead, he gently tucked the covers around her and kissed her temple. "I'm sorry, Alana," he whispered. "But it's better this way. You deserve much more than I have to give."

Feeling like he'd just torn his own heart from his chest, Noah quickly got dressed and quietly slipped away.

ALANA TRIED TO tell herself that she wasn't disappointed when she woke at eight-thirty to find cold sheets on Noah's side of the bed. He was long gone.

Had she really expected more from him? He'd told her about his childhood. He was probably very rattled about laying himself bare and wanted to put as much distance between them as possible.

No, she had not expected even that much from him. What she had expected was more from herself. She'd known what she was getting into. This knot of disappointment should not be lying heavily in her stomach. Noah was who he was, and she couldn't change him.

She wasn't sorry she'd slept with him, but she did feel a bit deflated. She'd started to have hopes of something she had no business hoping. Not with Noah. He'd never lied to her about who he was or what he wanted. The unrealistic expectations were totally hers.

It's okay. It's all right. Nothing wrong with a casual fling. Except she'd wanted so much more.

There. That was the problem. She and Noah wanted different things. Alana wanted a relationship and he...

Well, she had no idea what Noah wanted.

She got up, moving stiffly because of the sweet ache between her legs and took a shower. She got dressed, padded into the kitchen. She made breakfast and sat at the table, looking out over her backyard. Loneliness seeped into her bones. Resolutely, she pushed the feeling aside.

Her doorbell rang and her heart leapt. Noah! He'd come back.

She scurried to the door, opened it to find a man in a mechanic's shirt holding a tablet computer and her car keys.

"Alana O'Hara?"

"Yes."

"I've brought your car back to you. If you could just sign here." He held out the computer for an electronic signature.

She put a hand to her throat. "I don't understand."

"Noah Briscoe called me before dawn," he said. "Asked me to get out of bed, go to the police station and retrieve your vehicle. Said it was a rush job. Paid extra for me to get to work right away. It's parked in your driveway."

"Noah paid to have my car fixed?"

"Yes, ma'am. He thinks you're something special."

"He does?"

"I've been his mechanic for six years and I've never seen him like this."

"Like what?" Alana took the tablet he extended. Signed her name. Handed it back.

The mechanic smiled. "Head over heels."

"He's not head over heels for me," she corrected.

"He might not say it. Noah's tight-lipped." The man nodded. "But he shows it. Whenever he says your name his face lights up like a kid on Christmas."

A car horn tooted from the curb.

"Gotta go," the mechanic said. "That's my ride back to the shop."

"Thanks," Alana said and absentmindedly closed her door. Was it true? Could Noah really be head of over heels for her? Fresh hope rose up inside her, but she didn't want to deceive herself about their chances.

When she got to work, Dwight Jacoby met her in the lobby.

"They've officially arrested Teague Price for arson. Apparently new evidence has come to light and it's pretty damning. C'mon. Let's head over to the jail," he said, taking her by the elbow.

The second she saw Noah again, her stomach hitched. Their eyes met across the interrogation room table and she didn't hear a single word anyone said as she struggled to get a read on Noah.

He was totally closed off, body stiff, jaw set, shoulders squared. He gave no indication of what they'd shared the night before. He kept his expression neutral, everything focused on the interview. Of course, he was a professional. This was a job situation. He would not let on how he felt.

Still, his impervious stare sent an icy breeze over her.

Talk about mixed messages. On the one hand, he'd gotten up early and paid to have her car repaired. His actions—and what his mechanic told her—seemed to indicate that she was special to him. But his standoffish body language said something else entirely.

It wasn't until Dwight's hand touched her shoulder that Alana realized the interview was over and Teague Price was being led to a cell.

"You're a million miles away," Dwight said when as they left the interrogation room together. Alana had to force herself not to give Noah a parting glance over her shoulder. "Is something eating at you?"

Yes! Noah Briscoe. "He's guilty, isn't he?" She nodded in the direction the jailer had propelled Teague Price.

"Probably," Dwight said. "But our job is to mount the best defense."

"Even when we know for certain our clients are guilty?"

"Yes."

"Do you ever feel wrong about that? Helping guilty people get off?"

"Everyone is entitled to a fair defense. It's the prosecution's job to prove their case. If I'm better at my job than they are…" Dwight shrugged, held out his palms. "I win."

"Even though a criminal is free to roam the streets?'

Dwight paused, gave her a hard look. "You thinking about switching sides, Alana?"

She raised her chin. "I believe maybe I am."

"Why the attack of conscience?"

"My thinking has started shifting lately."

"Since you've been keeping company with a certain police officer?" Dwight raised his eyebrows. "Are you going to let a cop lure you to the dark side?"

She thought about the evening in the diner when Dwight had taken the Clausen case away from her so he could grandstand for the media. Her conversation that night with Noah was when her ideology had started to shift. She wanted to be on Noah's side. To help put the bad guys behind bars, not set them free.

"Yes," she said simply. "I am."

"It's just a phase you're going through," Dwight said. "Give it some time before you make a big decision like that. Don't base your career on a romantic fantasy."

"Alana," Noah called to her just as she and Dwight reached the exit. "Could I have a word with you?"

Heart pounding, she halted.

"I'll see you back at the office," Dwight said. "Remember, this is your future. Don't let your heart lead your head astray." He went out the door, leaving her alone in the corridor with Noah.

Her gut twisted when she saw he was frowning. "Hello," she said breathlessly, stupidly, as if they just hadn't spent the last twenty minutes together in interrogation.

"Did you get your car back okay?" he asked.

She nodded. "Thank you for arranging the repairs for me. I'll pay you back."

He waved a hand, but did not meet her gaze directly. "The car repairs are an apology."

"What—"

"Last night, I was completely out of line."

Was he apologizing for slipping out on her this morning? It was okay. She understood. Forgave him.

"We should never have… *I* should never have…" He paused. "Taken advantage of you the way I did."

He was withdrawing, backpedalling. He hadn't had her car fixed because she was special to him, but because he felt guilty. Stricken, Alana caught her breath. She was a good enough lawyer not to let her true feelings show. Couldn't let him see how he was wounding her. Besides, she'd known that Noah had issues. Making him feel badly about the situation was not the solution.

Determined to appear casual, she laughed. "Oh, Noah, don't beat yourself up. Last night was lots of fun, but I've got no expectations of anything more from you."

He splayed a palm to the nape of his neck. "You don't?"

"No." She shook her head, even though her heart was

breaking. "I do like spending time with you, but it doesn't have to mean anything."

"It doesn't?" He looked confused.

"Listen, I'll give you some time to think about whether you'd like to have a full-fledged fling or if one night together was enough. The Firemen's Ball is Christmas Eve. If you show up, we can spend the evening together. If not…" She shrugged. "No hard feelings."

"I…um… I have to work Christmas Eve."

"What time do you get off?"

"Six."

"The gala starts at eight."

"You know I don't do Christmas," he said. "It's why I volunteer to work the holidays."

"That's just the problem, isn't it? You've kept a stranglehold on the Christmas spirit for so long that you don't know how to let yourself be happy. You're punishing yourself for the past. It's over. You have to let go or you'll never find happiness."

"I…" He moistened his lips. "It's not that simple."

"It is that simple. All you have to do is make the effort. It's up to you, Noah. No pressure. No expectations. Do whatever makes you happy."

With that, she spun on her heel, anxious to get away. There was only so much playacting even a good lawyer could do.

7

THE STATION HOUSE was creepily quiet on Christmas Eve. Nothing was happening. Noah had spent the day thinking about what Alana had said the day he arrested Teague Price for arson.

She'd put the onus on him. She'd left him an out, but at the same time, she'd kept things open for a possible future. What did he want?

Alana.

That's what he wanted.

But he was so afraid to take that next step. To voice what he wanted. Needed. Vulnerability made him feel weak. To admit that he needed her...well, he might as well go into a gang fight without his vest and gun. Whenever he was around her, he felt stripped bare, as if she could see straight through him.

Rattled, he watched her walk away. He wanted more than anything in the world to call out to her, to tell her how he really felt. Being with her made him feel alive. Happy.

And happiness scared the hell out of him.

Much easier, much safer to take the out she'd offered him. He was not going to that ball. He couldn't face the holiday merriment.

Not even for a chance with Alana?

Hell, they were all wrong for each other. Total opposites. If she spent more time with him, soon enough Alana would realize they weren't well suited. Yeah, they were great in bed together. Yeah, he could talk to her more readily than anyone he knew. Yeah, she made him want to be a better man, but eventually, she'd want more than what he could give. She needed a guy who could match her cheery spirit. A guy who could tell her everything he was feeling. A guy without a dark side.

He was not that guy.

Better to just end it now before they both really got hurt.

It sounded good in his head, but his skin suddenly felt too tight as if he was a prisoner in his own body. He couldn't even sit still. He prowled the hallway looking for something to occupy his time. Found nothing. The case against Teague Price was going forward. The woman who'd been found unconscious in the Price Mansion, and who'd suffered from short-term amnesia as a result of her attack, had finally recovered her memory. Noah had taken her statement as she recalled visiting the mansion for old time's sake and that while she was there, she'd unexpectedly surprised Teague in the process of setting the fire. The case of who burned down the Price Mansion had been solved. He'd done his job.

Why then, was he so unfulfilled?

At six o'clock he bundled up in his overcoat. The thought of heading home alone to his empty apartment daunted him. The local cop bar was just a few blocks away. He could walk over and have a beer with all the other people who had nowhere special to be on Christmas Eve. The cool air might clear his head of these constant thoughts of Alana.

Snow started to fall as he left the station house. Perfect for Christmas Eve. The ground was slushy from an earlier snow that had melted off. Snowflakes danced from the sky, showering everything in a rain of soft white. They were turning Pine Crest into a schmaltzy holiday wonderland. Alana would love it.

By the time Noah reached the main thoroughfare, the stores were closing as shoppers hurried to their vehicles clutching packages. People called out "Merry Christmas" to one another. Holiday lights winked and twinkled from the buildings and street lamps.

Feeling like an interloper who'd somehow stumbled into the pristine world of a perfect snow globe, Noah stood on the street corner with his hands jammed into his pockets, waiting for the light to change. His lungs seized up. Not from the brisk air, but from the nagging sense of loss that gripped him.

By keeping Alana at arm's length, this was the kind of feeling he'd been trying to avoid. He'd lost so much. He was terrified of losing more.

But he'd already lost.

Lost Alana.

Lost his heart.

He had nothing but his job. No one to keep him warm at night. Nothing to come home to. No one to make him smile.

"Sergeant Briscoe."

Noah looked up, spied Christopher Clausen waving at him from the opposite street corner, looking jolly in his Santa costume. What a sharp contrast Clausen's bright smile was to Noah's dark thoughts.

"Miracles happen when you believe," Clausen called out to him and winked.

Yeah, right.

Suddenly, Noah wanted to believe. Wanted so badly to think he stood a chance with Alana. To embrace Christmas. To let the spirit of love and goodwill toward all mankind well up inside him until it spilled over. Wanted it so desperately that his lungs refused to expand.

Did Clausen have the answers?

Noah started to cross the intersection, to apologize to the man for the way he'd handled his arrest, but a furniture truck rumbled down the street between him and Clausen, blocking his view.

Once the truck had passed, Noah was startled to discover Clausen had disappeared.

Where could he have gone in those few seconds?

Miracles happen when you believe.

Noah's pulse jumped erratically. Had Clausen actually been there? Was he having hallucinations?

Miracles happen when you believe.

It was corny. Sentimental. Sappy. And yet…and yet…

His hope floated.

Inspired, and determined not to overthink the impulse that gripped him, Noah searched the town square. At the jewelry store cattycorner to where he stood, the shopkeeper was locking up.

"Wait!" Noah called out, sprinting across the street. "Please wait!"

The startled shopkeeper glanced up as Noah arrived, breathless and anxious. "I need a gift for my girlfriend," he said. "Could you open back up?"

"I'm closed." The shopkeeper shook his head.

"It's Christmas Eve," Noah said. "She's very special to me. I want…no, I need to get her something that tells her how I feel about her."

"Why did you wait so long to buy her a gift?" asked the shopkeeper, a goateed man in his early fifties who peered at Noah over the top of his glasses.

"Because I'm a big idiot."

The shopkeeper chuckled. "I've been there, I feel for you, but my family is waiting for me."

"I'll be quick. I promise," Noah vowed.

The shopkeeper hesitated.

"Please."

The man gave a good-natured sigh. "All right, but make it snappy."

Relief spread through Noah, but once inside the store, he looked around in confusion. So much to chose from. The gift had to be just right. Something that had meaning for both of them. Something that said he truly "got" her.

The shopkeeper tapped restlessly on the jewelry case.

"I know, I know." He didn't want to purchase something out of desperation. Maybe it was better if he just forgot the whole thing.

The shopkeeper cleared his throat, checked his watch.

Too much pressure. He was running out of time and if he hoped to make it to the Firemen's Ball on time, he needed to go home and change right now. Noah was just about to apologize to the shopkeeper when he spied it.

The perfect Christmas gift for Alana.

ALANA TRIED NOT to get her hopes up. She was stag at the Firemen's Ball, wearing a sapphire-blue dress that played up her eyes and auburn hair. The place was packed to the rafters. The dance floor was crowded. She waited near the entrance in order to catch a glimpse of Noah if he decided to show.

It's eight-thirty. He's not coming. Give it up already. Go find your friends. Have some fun.

Good advice, but she couldn't seem to make herself move away from the door.

Go!

Resolutely, she headed toward the buffet table loaded down with a Christmas Eve feast. She had to stop expecting anything from Noah. She couldn't change him. He was who he was.

"Alana."

She froze, the sound of Noah's voice in her ears. He'd come after all!

Alana turned around, her pulse hammering.

Noah stood there, snow melting in his hair, a long narrow box wrapped in foil paper the same color as her dress clutched in his hand. He wore a tuxedo and his face was clean-shaven. He looked so incredibly handsome. Her breath stilled in her lungs. His dark-eyed gaze, gentle and contrite, tracked over her face.

"You came," she whispered.

"Yeah," he said.

"Does this mean—"

"I want you, Alana. In my bed. In my life. In my heart." He paused, waited.

"Are you sure?"

"I've never been more certain of anything in my life," he vowed.

"You promise not to withdraw when things get bumpy? Because all relationships hit speed bumps. It doesn't mean anything is wrong. You have to learn how to navigate the speed bumps in order to have a relationship."

"I want to learn how to have an honest intimate relationship and I want to have it with you. Please teach me, Alana. I…" He swallowed and she could tell this was a huge step for him. "I need you."

She knew how difficult this was for him. He was taking a big chance. Putting his heart on the line for her. "You're serious."

"One hundred percent." He extended the gift-wrapped box toward her. "Open it."

She untied the silver ribbon, peeled open the pretty wrapping. Inside the box was a gold necklace with a scales-of-justice charm. She smiled and looked up.

He answered with a nervous smile of his own. "Read the inscription on the back."

She turned the charm over. *To Alana. My one and only. You balance me. Love, Noah.*

Love?

He was in love with her?

She raised her gaze to meet his once more. "Noah," she whispered.

"I mean it," he said. "You've brought me out of my self-imposed shell and into the light. I love how your warmth evens out my toughness. I love your joy for life. I love your fire and your spirit. I love you, Alana O'Hara. I've been in love with you for months. I'd never felt like this before and it scared me, so I tried to deny it, but I can't deny it any longer. I'm in love with you and I was hoping you feel the same way about me because I'm crazy for you and—"

"Shh." She pressed two fingers to his lips. "I'm crazy for you, too, Noah Briscoe. Now, come dance with me."

Alana led him to the dance floor. They swayed to the notes of "White Christmas," snow falling steadily outside the window, the spirit of the holidays burning in their hearts, and they both knew that this was the very Merriest Christmas of all.

* * * * *

KATHLEEN O'REILLY

BARING IT ALL

To all the readers and booksellers who have
filled my inbox with happiness and smiles.

1

THE GRAND PRICE Mansion was a smoldering mess of ash, disappearing right before his eyes. It was going to be one hell of a Christmas present for the town of Pine Crest, Virginia. Eric Marshall leaned against the ambulance, arms folded across his chest, and got comfortable because it looked to be a long night. The old mansion didn't have residents anymore, and the museum employees would be gone, so all that was left for his EMT crew to do was babysit the firemen, who as a rule were not a swift bunch and wouldn't recognize the signs of smoke inhalation if it reached and out and bit 'em in the ass. He watched as the fire chief leaned out of the ground-floor window and motioned for the hose. To be fair, it took guts to run into a burning building, risking life and limb to save human lives, canine lives, feline lives, rodent lives, beaten-up teddy bear lives, and the worst offender of them all: the ever-popular Christmas presents. Yup, it definitely took lots of guts and not a lot of brains. However, some of Eric's best friends were firemen, so he kept his opinion of their mental capacities to himself.

Clouds of water sent the smoke plumes dancing out into the cold winter night. The crews were blasting the half-standing first floor, but the second story was gone. He knew the house, had played there some as a kid, and it felt strange to see the piece of his past disappear. To see the piece of Virginia state history disappear, too. The fabled homestead of Virginia's most favored governor, Colin T. Price.

And there was already a crowd of rubberneckers huddled out in the road. Wyatt from the barbershop in a black parka over flannel pajamas. The waitress from the diner, whose name he always forgot. There was old Mrs. Tidwell, who had been the principal of Pine Crest Middle School for four generations. Tonight, everybody had come out for the drama, even Santa Claus.

"Got any marshmallows?" asked Henry, the second lieutenant at the Pine Crest Volunteer Ambulance Corps. Henry was a tough old bird, with a head as bald as a vulture, and drove the bus like a blind Mario Andretti.

"Too much sugar will kill you," lectured Eric, because as a state-licensed health official, he was supposed to know these things, and also because he liked to give Henry hell.

Henry considered it, scratching at the gray stubble on his jaw. "Don't matter once you get to my age. Life isn't worth living without a vice or two. Not giving up the cigars, but I can give up the sugar. The trick is to find a substitute." He paused, and Eric waited, because Henry talked in fits and starts. "Hey, after we're done here, how about a slice of pizza? I bet you could sweet-talk Alyssa into opening up the place and baking us a sweet-smelling pile of artery-clogging ambrosia. Extra cheese, some mushrooms, sautéed onions."

Alyssa was the owner of Cicero's Pizza Pies and had spent one summer delivering a lot more to Eric than pizza. It wasn't a relationship he was particularly proud of, but since he didn't have a relationship he was particularly proud of, Eric didn't lose sleep over the matter.

Nope, in fact, he had perfect blood pressure at one-ten over seventy, a steady heart rate of sixty BPM, and a cholesterol level of one-seventy. Every part of Eric Marshall was perfectly tuned to remain cold and detached, no matter the emergency, no matter the crisis. It was part of the Marshall family DNA.

The purr of a tightly tuned Mercedes twin-turbo engine whispered in the commotion, and he felt his blood pressure spike. "Give me a minute," he said to Henry.

"Family reunions are always fun. Give your father a hug from me, will you?"

Eric looked at the older man and glared. "Bite me."

Then his eyes cut to where Santa Claus was standing, and Eric wondered whose holiday party had broken up early. Over the years, the Pine Crest ambulance had carted more St. Nicks to the hospital than Eric cared to remember. Most were the mall rent-a-wrecks, walking the fine line between "ho-ho-ho" and "put the mentally unstable man on meds." In Eric's professional opinion, a Santa Claus was a medical emergency waiting to happen, and it seemed irresponsible to ignore the impending disaster right in front of him.

Besides, he loved to piss off his dad.

He made his way to Santa and coughed politely, but Santa's attention was firmly fixed on the house.

"They could be hours here," Eric said to him. "You should get home, Santa."

The old man adjusted his wire glasses, the reflection of the fire giving an odd light to his eyes. "I go where I'm needed, son. Just like you."

Eric laughed, the smoke turning what should have been a happy sound into something like a death rattle. "I think the holiday eggnog has been fogging your brain."

"She's running away from the man she loves." The old man turned to Eric. "You have to help her."

Startled by the nonsense words, Eric scanned the pupils of Santa, looking for signs of narcotics or stroke. "How're you feeling there?"

In response, Santa gave him the patient yet still patroniz-ing smile reserved for the kids with coal in their stockings. "You have to help her. She's going to need you."

She? Who was she? Santa was talking extra loopy tonight. He looked to be in decent physical shape, except for the extra seventy pounds around the stomach. That would be killer on the heart. Eric nodded, and gave him the patient yet still pa-tronizing smile reserved for patients who weren't all there. "Who are we talking about?"

"Her." Santa nodded toward the smoking grounds. The front hall of the grand Victorian had been salvaged, but there was a big open-air sunroom where the back half used to be. The stained-glass windows had been knocked out, the plastic Christmas tree was nothing more than melted wax on a pole and there were four antique Chippendale chairs on the lawn. Among all the other wreckage, there was no "her." As the first responders on call, they would have known.

Right then, the emergency radio at his hip started to beep, and he heard the shouts. "We've got a survivor."

Forgetting about Santa, his father and his general dis-like for the whole holiday whackadoo, Eric raced to the ambulance, ready to do his job. After she was loaded in the back, Henry climbed behind the wheel, and Eric checked the patient's airway, breathing and pulse. Not too bad, considering the long exposure to smoke. The breathing was shallow, but there weren't any burn marks around her mouth. With steady hands, he placed the mask on her face, opening the oxygen valve and letting the concen-trated air do its work.

Santa had been right. It was a "her." Late twenties. Uncon-scious. Nasty laceration on the back of her head, which was almost white from gray dust. Plaster, not soot. A lot of plaster that probably saved her life. While the quiet hiss of the unit pumped air into her lungs, he measured the CO_2 blood lev-

els. He was relieved to see the red LEDs flash almost normal.
With the ambulance doors shut, there were so few sounds that
Eric could watch her color, the chalky gray slowly receding
to show signs of recovery.

She wasn't from Pine Crest. He would have known the face.
Eric knew all the females in Pine Crest, had slept with a number of them at one time or another. As her breathing steadied
and she began to regain consciousness, her hands clawed at
the oxygen mask. He noticed the huge wedding ring on her
finger. He didn't sleep with the married ones, because there
were some lines he wouldn't cross, unlike his father.

He brushed at her hand, gently placing it back down at
her side, and wide blue eyes stared, nervous, scared and red-
rimmed from the fire.

"It's all right. You're in an ambulance. We're going to Pine
Crest General."

Her mouth opened and closed, trying to talk. Too much
smoke could be hell on the throat. "You don't need to say anything," he told her. "It might hurt."

Once again the lips moved. "No hurt talk."

"What's your name?" he asked, re-checking the pulse. It
was accelerated, but not alarming.

She opened her mouth. Closed her mouth. "I'm…I'm…"
she started before trailing off.

"I'm…"

He shook his head. "Don't talk. Seriously. I'm not the chatty
type. You won't offend me at all."

"I'm…" She closed her eyes and frowned.

"You're in pain?"

She nodded.

"Your head?"

Another nod.

Eric smoothed back the dusty hair from her face and then
examined the back of her head. The plaster dust had done

the same work as a bandage, and dried blood was matted to her head. Not exactly high fashion or Johns Hopkins, but it had done a fine job clotting the wound, not so great at calming the fear.

It was there in her eyes. Her pupils were dilated, her gaze fused with his as if she needed his strength. Big, sloppy tears of more than pain welled at the corners of her eyes. He could read the fear there as well, and he wished that he could take away her pain and take away the fear. It wasn't quite the cool efficiency that he was so proud of. Not that he needed to worry too much, because once they admitted her to the hospital, his job was done. Over. Kaput. That was the beauty of EMS. Standard operating protocol: treat, transport and take off. Once she was admitted to the hospital, he'd never see her again. Not a problem, because yes, he reminded himself, she belonged to somebody else.

But what had Santa told him? That she was running away. That Eric was supposed to help her. Not that he was going to believe Santa Claus. But what if she was in trouble? Did she really need him, or had Santa been messing with more than a little pixie dust? At that moment, with her wide eyes chained to his, he could feel all her messy emotions rolling through him, like a Vulcan mind meld.

Oh, yeah, Henry would laugh about that one.

But not Santa. Santa wouldn't be surprised at all, and Eric, who didn't believe in Santa, didn't believe in messing in other people's lives, found himself deciding to help her. Because she needed him, this woman with the pleading eyes.

"What's your name?" he asked, because he wanted to know. He wanted to know her first name, her last name, where she lived, and what she was running from. Suddenly, Eric was full of questions, just as curious as the proverbial cat—the one that got killed.

Her brows pulled together, her eyes closed, and when she opened them up, the pain was back, worse, as was the fear.

"I...don't...know."

THE HOSPITAL ROOM was white. Too much white. White curtains, white sheets, white walls, white tile. It was so white that it hurt her eyes, or maybe it was the construction crew that was pounding in her brain. They needed color in this room. Bright yellow curtains, or maybe a cobalt blue.

When she tried to sit up, the room started to spin and she fell back in the bed. It was only a few inches, but it felt like twenty stories onto brick. And the jackhammers in her head were back.

Ouch.

"The doc said you have a minor concussion. Not sure why they say minor. I bet it hurts like hell. But you're here. You're safe."

It was the voice, the sandpaper voice from the ambulance. Her eyes felt heavy, like two grand pianos were balanced on top of each one, but she opened them anyway, because she wanted to see the face.

It was almost familiar to her, especially his eyes. Cement-gray eyes, and just as hard. He was sitting in a corner chair, a plastic thing...white, of course. And he looked tired. And wired. Like when you stayed up too late and wanted to sleep but couldn't sleep because there was music playing and people were laughing and you weren't supposed to stay up late, but you couldn't look away.

He tried to smile at her, the corner of his mouth lifting, but he didn't do it well. She wasn't sure why he was unhappy. He looked healthy, no minor concussion, no jackhammers, and to top it all off, he probably liked the color white. She experienced a weird desire to hit him, and she wondered if that was from the headache, too. Probably.

Deciding all that anger wasn't helping her head, she glanced down, focusing on the newspaper on the floor at his feet. "Pine Crest."

"You remember that?" he asked, leaning forward, elbows balanced on strong thighs. He was still wearing the white medic's shirt from last night, but there were black smudges across his chest. He didn't belong in such pedestrian clothes. His perfectly proportioned frame needed something elegant and sophisticated. A tuxedo. He would be hot in a tux. Whoa. Waves of heat skimmed over her nerves, and she wondered if headaches inspired lust, too. If she was lucky, this was nothing more than a fever.

The cement eyes were looking at her curiously.

"What?" she asked.

"You remember where you are?"

"I'm at the hospital," she answered, surprised at the idiotic question because he looked very smart.

"Pine Crest. You remember Pine Crest?"

She blinked, trying to place the name. It was there in her mind, but she didn't understand why it was there. "Not exactly."

He leaned forward. "Yes or no?"

Not a patient man, which didn't bode well for his bedside manner. Of course, medics weren't required to have bedside manners. They only carried patients to the hospital and then went on to the next sick person. Except for this one. It was nice that he had stayed on to be with her. Assuming that he had stayed on to be with her.

"Why are you here?"

"Paperwork. The state likes to know who rides in the ambulance so they can bill you, or your insurance company. They're not particular."

Oh. It was only business. She had hoped that it was something more. She closed her eyes because jackhammers didn't belong in the brain. And now there was a hammer in her chest as well. Not just a headache, but a fever and a heart attack, too. God, she was going to be lucky to walk out of this hospital alive.

"And I made a promise to take care of you."

Slowly she opened her eyes, one at a time, in case his words were a feverish hallucination. However, there was a sexy flush on his cheeks and she didn't think she would be hallucinating flushes. Other things, yes. A passionate tango down the hospital hall, slipping champagne in her IV bag or throwing rose petals on the floor of the zero-threshold accessible walk-in shower. These were the sorts of hospital fantasies she would have created, not an awkward blush...or the way the cement eyes had softened, but only a bit.

"I don't remember you promising to take care of me." That, she would have remembered.

"You don't remember much."

"I remember the fire. And the heat. It was hot, smelting hot, like it was the end of the world, and the jaws of hell had opened to devour everything in their path." She could still feel the heat on her face, and the flickering flames of the fire, and the fear...knowing that each breath might be her last.

"Did you see how the fire started?" he asked, ignoring the high-drama parts, and moving on to the mundane. She had thought he would have appreciated her reliving the terror of her last moments alive—but no. He was probably practical, which she supposed was a good quality in a paramedic.

When she drew in a breath, it wasn't so easy, and she frowned.

"You saw something?" he prodded.

"No. It hurts to breathe."

"Sorry about that. There was a four by four on your chest. That and the piece of wall plaster kept you alive."

"A four by four?"

"A big post."

She scoffed. "I know what a four by four is."

"How?"

Then she blinked, trying to orient herself in the past, but nothing came to her mind. No pictures, no names, no memories. Nothing. "I don't know."

"You were banged up from the wall. Lots of bruises. It's not going to be pretty for a while."

Bruises? That explained the pain in her chest. She pulled the hospital gown away from her skin, and glanced down to see two particularly great breasts completely ruined by the ugly mass of purple that blanketed her torso. Damn. No plunging cleavage anytime soon.

"Don't worry. Take your time. Heal. Your memory will come back."

It was nice that he believed that it was her memory loss that was bugging her. But she hadn't gotten that far. Right now it was the little discoveries. Relief that she had a killer body. That her brain still worked. It felt good. Powerful. Freeing. She wanted to explore that freedom. She wasn't sure that she wanted her memories back. What if they were average? Or worse than average? What if she was boring? What if she worked in—God forbid—insurance? Somehow the bruises, the headaches, the tubes in her arm were preferable to the other, and she wasn't sure why she didn't want to think about who she was. It wasn't fear, like being in witness protection, or running from the Mafia. Instead, it was the low thrum of anxiety, the fear of being discovered for who you really are. But again, these sorts of personality quirks weren't what she was going to confess to the generous man who had just promised to take care of her. These sorts of personality quirks were what drove men away from her. "Maybe it's better if I don't remember."

"You have someone back home who won't be happy if you never remember."

"How do you know?"

"You had a wedding ring on when they pulled you out."

A wedding ring? Wouldn't she remember a husband, a family, a wedding? Walking down the aisle with a twenty-yard train, and a string quartet playing the wedding march? The dress was vivid in her mind, a fitted waist, a scallop of lace over her chest, a diamond-studded veil. The dress would have cost a fortune. Over twenty thousand if done right. What if she was rich? She didn't feel rich. *Or married.* "I should remember a husband."

"Maybe you don't want to remember him."

She met his eyes, tried to read his meaning, but wasn't sure. He was being deliberately vague. He liked doing that, teasing her with things just out of reach. "Don't say that."

"You're right. Odds are you're happily married, traveling to a strange town for the holidays, getting caught in a deserted house and almost killed. I completely get that."

Sarcasm was never pretty, especially since she was the victim-amnesiac-chick with the sexy body. Men were supposed to really go for that. "Are you always like this?"

"Yes," he answered with the sort of self-aware smile that comes from a man who knows his own personality quirks, and really doesn't care what the world thinks about them. But people always cared. At some level, even when they pretended not to care, what the world thought always mattered.

"So how is it that you promised to take care of me? It seems out of character."

He laughed, and not in a happy way. "It is."

"Forget about the promise. Go home. Get some sleep. You're officially off the case." She jabbed at the call button next to her bed. "I hurt. I think I want to be alone."

"I'm sorry."

"Sorry doesn't fix everything."

"No. But I'm worried about you."

"Why?"

"I don't know. You're alone. You were scared last night. You don't remember, and what if you're running away from something?"

"Like the Russian Mafia or a drug cartel?" She closed her eyes, drew a blank on any guns, drugs or the IRS. "I don't think so."

"Statistically it's very unlikely it's something that dramatic. Probably you had a fight with your husband. That's why women run away."

"You had a lot of them run from you, did you?" she teased.

"Not a one."

"Not very smart, are they?"

An older nurse poked her head in the door, the pink flowered scrubs a happy change from the suffocating white walls. "How are you feeling?" Then she turned to the man in the chair. "Eric, you shouldn't be here."

Eric. His name was Eric. Eric Marshall. She didn't know why she knew his full name. The night of the fire, she must have read it on his badge. "I'll leave," he was saying, unfolding himself from the chair, and she realized he was taller than she had assumed. He didn't carry himself like other men, he didn't stride, or pose. Instead, he always seemed to want to fade into the walls, except a man like that never could.

"Goodbye, Eric. Have a nice life."

He moved to the door, giving her an odd look. Not angry, not insulted, more tolerant than she would have expected. "I'll be here after dinner."

The nurse swallowed her laugh and unwound the blood-pressure cuff from the stand. "Doesn't sound like a good idea, Eric."

She wasn't sure what they meant, but she noticed the look

of warning that the nurse shot the man. "You don't have to come back. I'll be great."

She knew he felt responsible for her, and she wasn't sure why, and it irked her. She knew he desired her, and she wasn't sure why, and it thrilled her.

He looked at the nurse. "Paperwork. You ever tried to turn in a PCR without the patient's name?" Then he turned to her and shrugged. "Sorry."

And he didn't look sorry in the least.

2

CHLOE SKIDMORE.

It had to be. She was older. She was a helluva lot skinnier, but the run-on mouth hadn't changed. The wild imagination hadn't changed either.

So was she faking the memory loss? Fake amnesia would have been exactly the sort of high-drama tactics that Chloe used to love, but Eric didn't think so.

Chloe Skidmore.

Damn.

Her father had been the caretaker of the Price Mansion for nearly thirty years, a sort of English butler wannabe who drank too much and kissed too much green-backed ass. But not Chloe. No, that was one female who had never met a member of the town's first families that she wouldn't try to out-fox. Which would have worked great in a bigger place—where people didn't know Chloe—or didn't know Buddy Skidmore, her dad. But in Pine Crest, all the kids knew Chloe, knew that she had as much kick as a one-legged mule. And so it was written that Chloe Skidmore had been blown off every day that ended in *y*. Not that he was going to feel guilty, because it was Chloe's mouth that got her in trouble, not Eric. Her lush, cherry-ripe mouth that had always opened a little bit too far.

While Eric drove to the ambulance building, he wondered what had brought Chloe back to Pine Crest. Revenge? Enough to burn down the old mansion? No. The cops had already cleared her, because whoever had started the fire had removed the accelerant.

Maybe it was the husband.

The husband.

Damn. In his triple-X fantasies, he could imagine that pale body wrapped around some lucky man. The way she had wrapped around him that one Christmas twelve years ago in a first-class stupid move; he had sworn her to secrecy after their night in the wine cellar of the mansion. Lots of guys would have bragged about sex—lots of guys including Eric—but a man couldn't brag about being with Chloe, because Chloe was different.

Chloe was fat.

Not that she hadn't been hot. At sixteen, with the snow-flake skin, the bodacious breasts and the cherry nipples that had budded to life under his tongue, lots of guys had joked about getting with Chloe. Nobody had, except one.

His cock remembered that night like it was yesterday, and he glanced at the car next to him, feeling a set of all-knowing eyes watching him, but there wasn't anybody there. Only his conscience was at work.

Was there anything worse than a guilty conscience with a hard-on? No, Eric didn't think so. His foot hit the accelerator, needing to move past this.

A car horn blared.

Eric slammed on the brakes.

The mayor was driving the tiny red Toyota, glaring at him as if he were nuts.

Because he was nuts.

He flicked a halfhearted wave of apology, then glued his

eyes to the stoplight, because if he wrecked the ambulance, Henry would never let him live it down.

Once safely back at the ambulance building, Eric parked the rig in the bay, and adjusted his still-aching privates. Inside, the day crew was playing "Halo III."

"Tracy resigned. Sucks for you." That was from Lily, a skinny high-schooler who loved drama, especially when blood loss was involved. She was going to go into nursing. Eric figured it was better than becoming a serial killer. "She left the holiday decorating manual in your box."

Eric frowned, knowing that, yes, he was screwed, but not wanting to go down without a fight, especially to a girl. Christmas decorations were not the job of the captain of the ambulance corps. They were the job of the hospitality secretary. A job relegated to the most junior member, like Lily for instance.

Not that she would want it, because every year the Pine Crest Ladies Auxiliary made Christmas decorations and gave them to the corps. One year's worth of decorations would have made it okay, but no, they owned forty years' worth of decorations. They had boxes of cottonball snowmen, most missing their balls. And who could forget the hand-painted ceramic Santas with American flags stamped on their bag o' presents? The gold, spray-painted angels had held up well because apparently spray-paint was the world's best preservative. When all the boxes were unpacked, the ambulance building turned into the showplace of Crafty Holiday Hell.

"I'm giving the job to Raul," Eric pronounced, because after all, he was captain. Ergo, he was the boss.

"He and Maureen are driving up to Vermont tomorrow. Won't be back until after the New Year." Lily smiled, like an angel—or a sociopath.

Eric pretended to consider the possibilities. "We can do without the decorations this year, or maybe scale back…"

"Ladies Auxiliary will have your ass atop their tree, painted in a festive green and red. And that's in a good year. Now that the Price Mansion is decimated, they're more holiday-crazed than ever. The charity ball committee has been meeting around the clock, and every idea gets nuttier than the last. No doubt about it, this year Christmas is going to be a holiday to remember. The mayor gave five-thousand-dollar checks to all emergency agencies that we're ordered, yes, ordered, to spend on even more ornamentation."

"I don't need this now."

"Is there ever a good time for an orgy of holiday decadence?" asked Henry, not looking up from the video game.

At the words *orgy* and *decadence,* Eric's brain rewound to Chloe, as did his privates. Smoothly he grabbed a clipboard from the captain's desk, holding it in front of his groin. "I'll be upstairs."

"You'll do it?" Lily asked.

Eric considered the idea, and wanted to reject it, but with the now-married Chloe Skidmore in town, sans memory, sans husband, a nightmare of holiday overload would be the perfect way to keep his mind and his libido on ice.

"Sure," he agreed, without any trace of holiday cheer. That was what the eggnog was for.

"Ho-ho-ho. Can't wait to watch this one, Captain, or should I call you Captain Sugarplum?" Lily chuckled to herself and Eric dashed for the stairs, visions of sugarplums spiking his pulse. He told himself it was sugarplums, not Chloe. Not Chloe at all.

SHE LOOKED BETTER this morning, less nervous. Her dark hair had been washed and hung in long, loose curls that made her sexier than any woman should be while wearing a butt-ugly blue hospital gown. Eric had hoped that the clear light of day would have shaken off some of the more carnal images that haunted his dreams, but no, even with her in a hospital bed, he was still struck with that tidal wave of hunger that centered around Chloe. Damn.

"Welcome back. I thought you would have deserted me."

Chloe greeted him with the cheery wave of someone who had no clue that she was the object of his late-night fantasies, including one especially weird one involving a topless elf costume and a chimney.

"Why would I desert you?" asked the man who had deserted her twelve years ago. Mentally he put the top back on the elf costume.

She's married.

"I don't know why I thought that. Just a feeling." Her blue eyes watched him, curiously, cautiously, and yet…there was something else there. In the past, she had called him names, "Alistair McSnobbyballs" being the favorite. But in those dangerous blue eyes was the same bold awareness that she watched him with now. Brave, stupid, blood-pumping hot. Eric looked away.

He settled into the uncomfortable plastic chair and put the wretched shopping bags behind him. "Do you remember anything?"

"No?" Her brow arched. The Chloe that he had known had spent hours trying to arch a brow, but never had any luck. Obviously somewhere down the line she'd figured it out. "Should I remember anything?"

"What did the doc say?" Eric knew that brain injuries were a crapshoot. Sometimes the mind protected itself from pain, and sometimes it was just a matter of the brain getting knocked in the wrong place. If he had been a nicer kid to her, he would have told the doc his suspicions about her identity and let them all sort it out. On the other hand, his suspicions could be wrong.

Maybe she wasn't Chloe. Maybe Santa Claus was a real

person. Maybe Eric wasn't such a jerk. Oh, yeah, all were possibilities. Not.

"Doing a little Christmas shopping there, Mr. Grinch?"

He looked down at the bag full of tinsel, relieved for the diversion but wishing he'd been out hunting or fishing or doing he-man sorts of things. He twisted his mouth in a Grinchy sort of smile. "Knee-deep in decorating hell. Don't ask."

She grinned, looking completely unashamed. "Now I have to know."

"Don't make me tell."

"You'd really deny such a small, completely sadistic pleasure to a woman who was in a fire, lost her memory, has no means of financial support? Only five days from Christmas? Seriously?"

He sighed, kicking at the larger bag with his boot.

"The hospitality secretary quit the corps this year. She was having a fight with the treasurer after he criticized her. He held up quote fingers, and said, 'World's worst chocolate cake,' and so she resigned. God bless volunteers."

Her laugh wasn't exactly the font of human goodness, but there was a rasp in her voice that made it…stimulating. That, and the challenge in her eyes. So different from the fear in the ambulance last night. "Nobody else left but you?"

"There's Mrs. Randolph and the Ladies Auxiliary," he tossed out the name, waiting for a sign of recognition. Finding none, he continued. "But they're working on the Firemen's Annual Christmas Eve Charity Ball. Now that the mansion is gone, every holiday nutjob in Pine Crest is determined to keep the ball happening. Idiots." He pulled a grinning Christmas elf from the bag, and watched a delighted smile show up on her face. He wasn't sure if she was happy with his foolishness, or the idea of the holidays, but either way, it didn't bother him like it should have.

"So you ended up with the sticky end of the candy cane?"

She hadn't meant it suggestively. He knew that with every inch of his being, but parts of his being took it that way and grew six inches. Discreetly he put the elf on his lap. "Ha. Ha."

She was married.

The married woman grinned as mischievously as the elf. "I suppose I should apologize for making fun of your misery, but the docs told me that being surly is allowed with a head injury." Apparently she thought the pain on his face was from embarrassment. Somehow it was easier that way.

"How are you feeling today?" There. Guide the conversation toward something impersonal and non-sexual.

"Definitely hurting, because you know I wouldn't be surly otherwise."

"Definitely."

"Sarcasm? Why is there sarcasm?"

"I don't know. Just a feeling."

She watched him suspiciously. "Is there something I should know?"

"Nope. Not a thing."

"Good, because you'd tell me, right?"

"Definitely."

He didn't think she believed him, but she was smart enough to not call him on it. The younger Chloe would have charged ahead, damn the torpedoes, and called him a liar. But apparently this new Chloe was older and wiser. And so much more untouchable.

"They're discharging me tomorrow," she announced.

Discharging her? "To where?"

"Dr. Montessano told me about the Bunratty Hotel down on Elm. I thought I could stay there. Of course, paying for it might be a problem until I have some sort of ID and money, but until then…I'll manage."

Oh, yeah. Right. Old Iron Claw Bunratty wasn't big on the whole "kindness of strangers" thing. Even at Christmas. "I can get you some assistance from the town. We have a fund for that." Yes, there was a fund. It was called Eric Marshall's checking account, but he wasn't going to tell her that.

"That's very generous of you."

"The town, not me," he corrected, because he didn't want her to think the wrong thing about the situation. He didn't want her to think that he was some white knight who ran around giving money to the ladies. Hell, that just sounded creepy. No, better for her to think that she was relying on the goodwill of the town. Besides, Pine Crest had treated Chloe like crap in the past, it only seemed right that they pay restitution, even if it was Eric funding the effort.

She was quiet for a while, nervous fingers plucking at the sheets. He wished that he knew where she belonged now, who she belonged to, but Eric knew that he shouldn't get involved. Bad idea. Rotten idea. And, of course, that idea was only reinforced when she looked up at him and he could feel something pull at his insides. A hernia would have been nice, but he didn't think he was that lucky.

"I hate this," she said, only twisting his insides more. "The not knowing. The idea of being in a hotel room. At Christmas. God knows, they probably don't even have a tree."

The Bunratty Hotel had a tree. They had a huge twenty-foot tree that they put up every year on Thanksgiving. And lots of greenery and ornaments, and not a single silly grinning elf to be found. It was the perfect place for her, and he should have told her that—but he didn't.

At his silence, she held up the remote to the television and clicked on a morning cooking show. Eric listened quietly while the hostess walked the studio audience through the fine art of baking a life-size gingerbread house. Chloe pulled her mouth into a tight line and changed the channel. On the next station, some bubbly blonde news announcer was broadcasting from a sleigh with eight dogs dressed up with antlers. Chloe clicked the remote again. Now some preschool kids were singing "Jingle Bells."

Chloe clicked the television off.

"I would know if I had a family, wouldn't I? I would know if I was a mother? I don't feel like a mother."

Did she feel like a wife? The words stuck on his tongue, but Chloe railed on, as if it wasn't even a part of the equation.

"It sucks. I don't want to stay in a hotel. Not for the holidays. I want to be in a place where there's people and presents and songs about snow. I want to be able to make gingerbread men and if I'm hungry, then I'll bite off their heads. I don't want to be alone at Christmas. I don't want to be by myself."

She met his eyes, and hers were full of that needy, don't-let-me-be-alone thing, and it was the same look she'd given him twelve years before. As a kid, he'd been enough of an ass to walk away, and without Chloe being around, it had been easy to think that it was no big deal.

But it was a big deal. He'd spent a long time shoving those memories into a dark closet where only skeletons and mix tapes mingled together. God, he'd been an ass. Totally befitting the Marshall name.

But not this time, he promised himself. He would make up for the past, give her a Christmas to remember until her memory came back. Before she realized who she was, and she remembered the name of the man she had married, or before she remembered exactly what Eric had done.

No, this time he wouldn't bail, which, considering her married condition, very ironically made him an even bigger ass than before. Guilt and lust were hell on a man's thinking, and guilty lust? Well, better men than Eric would have been just as stupid.

"You can bunk with me," he offered.

"Excuse me?" Her brows rose, surprise, shock, and yes,

apparently he wasn't the only one with a mind in the gutter. But at least she was calling him on it. Dammit.

Eric pretended to be shocked as well. "Not that way. I have a lot of extra space."

"So why do you look like your dog just died?"

There were two options here. Tell her the truth and confess his less-than-admirable intentions, even though they weren't actually intentions, more…ideas, or act like a total moron and make her believe that he didn't want her under his roof, and it was only some weird, "feed the poor, shelter the homeless" duty that had made him ask.

Eric chose the middle ground, neither admitting nor denying his lust, or his guilt. He sighed the patient, burdened sigh of a martyr. "It's okay. I'll be fine."

"You'd take in a complete stranger?"

"I made a promise," he explained, as if that made him an honorable person.

Her mouth tightened into a thin line. "There it is again, that pesky Christmas promise that seems to make you miserable. Listen, it's very nice of you, but I don't want to put you and your family out."

"Family?" Martyrdom momentarily forgotten, he looked at her, confused.

"Yes. Kids, dogs, or maybe y'all are a fish family. A wife."

He noticed the way she slid the reference in. Subtle, yes, but the look in her eyes was just like the Chloe he'd always known, budding with ideas that should have been extinguished a long time ago. His pulse raced like a man who lived for danger, except that wasn't Eric. He was the sensible one, the smart one. The one who didn't race into burning buildings, or invite helpless married women to bunk at his house. Except for one woman. This one.

Get up and leave, the sensible man told himself. *Make an excuse and get the hell out of her life.* But those eyes…a siren's eyes, the devil's eyes. With Chloe, it had always been the same, and once again, Eric Marshall was dying to touch the now-untouchable Chloe Skidmore.

"I don't have a family," he answered lightly.

"I'm sorry."

"Don't be. My parents are still alive, living on five beautifully manicured acres, and giving me hell for not practicing law. But there's no wife and kids—or fish. I'm not married."

"Oh." She sounded pleased, which pleased him. Then she glanced down at her left hand, remembering that she shouldn't be pleased. "I can't do that."

"I'm not around much," he countered, because she'd always had more street sense.

"Girlfriend?"

A girlfriend would have given him the perfect excuse. A demanding, jealous fiancée. "Ambulance corps," Eric answered instead. "Twenty-four seven, seven days a week, because emergencies don't sleep."

"You bunk at the building?"

"Most of the time." Not even close to the truth, but she needed a place to stay. He wanted to make up for the past. It seemed like a win-win.

She pushed back the dark hair from her face, and he was startled by the delicateness of her profile. She'd always been so touchy, so invincible, but something in the accident, or her life, had taken that away.

"You're very dedicated," she told him, as if he was a hero.

"Nah. Just have a lot of empty time on my hands." Because he was no hero. Far from it. The grinning elf in his lap looked up at him and agreed.

There was a knock at the door. They would be serving lunch, and Eric knew it was time to go. Pine Crest was small and people would talk. "I'll find out what time you're being discharged and pick you up tomorrow."

Then he left before she had a chance to disagree.

3

WEDNESDAY DAWNED bright and cold and full of new possibilities. She was dying to get out of the hospital and explore the town.

Eric had brought her some clothes to change into. A set of jeans, a sweatshirt and a coat, along with a matching set of bright yellow bra and panties. They weren't sexy enough for her to be insulted, but the bra was the perfect size. She chose not to ask.

Once outside, they trudged over the slushy ground where the last snowfall was stubbornly refusing to leave. She blinked against the glare of the sun on the snow, studying this place, Pine Crest, Virginia. What had drawn her here? It seemed tantalizingly familiar, but it could have been any of a thousand small towns decorated for the season. The streetlights were trimmed with red and green bells, and a Salvation Army bell ringer was greeting passersby with a cheery "Merry Christmas." In spite of her frustration, she smiled. She liked Christmas. That much, she knew.

On the way to his house, she watched his profile, his strong hands on the wheel, curious about who he really was, and what he knew of her. He was careful not to give away too much, and sometimes she wondered if he was the man who had put the ring on her finger. But that didn't make sense. Dr. Montessano would have told her.

She knew that Eric watched her. She could feel the weighty tension of his gaze, feel the intimacy that it contained. Her skin bloomed wherever he looked, like a winter crocus opening to the sun. Whatever the truth was between them, she knew things had happened. A woman knew when a man had touched her, even a woman with no memory.

Idly she twisted the gold band on her finger, trying to recall a husband, a wedding day, a lazy honeymoon in some exotic destination, but there were no memories, only a black cloud.

"You okay?" he asked.

"I should have a name."

"You do have a name."

Ah, yes. Eric, master of the obvious. "They called me Jane at the hospital. I hate the name Jane. It's very plain."

"You want something fancier?"

"More mysterious. More dramatic."

"Sasha? Or Cassandra? Not everybody is lucky enough to pick a new name."

"What would you call me?"

"Honey, baby or sweetheart. That's my go-to answer for unknown women."

"You have a talent for insulting the female sex?"

"I do."

"Come on. Help me out. What would you call me?"

He hesitated, and she waited for an answer. Waited for a name.

"Zoe," he answered. "You could be a Zoe."

"Zoe," she repeated, testing it out on her tongue. It sounded good, almost familiar. "Is that my name?"

He shot her a sideways glance, more than a little defensive. "How the hell should I know?"

"How the hell should you?" she shot back, with only a pinch of healthy skepticism. "You like your questions, don't you?"

"Do I?"

She crossed her arms over her chest, leaned back in the soft leather seat. "Go to hell."

He laughed. "I figure that's my eventual destination."

I figure that's my eventual destination. She knew those words. She knew the self-deprecating mockery of that tone, but the past was somewhere just beyond her reach. Like the man beside her, or the man who had placed the ring on her hand. All she knew was the twist of knots inside her, the pain in her head and the way she couldn't keep her eyes off Eric.

Hell. She figured that was *her* eventual destination, too.

BUYING CHRISTMAS decorations should have been a trip through the seventh ring of hell. Instead, it was, God help him, fun.

Chloe was a compulsive holiday shopaholic, and he found himself saying "yes" to the blow-up lawn Santa. He said "yes" to the spinning penguin ornaments. He said "yes" to the reindeer antlers that attached to the hood of the ambulance. Honestly, he should have put his foot down on the Santa toilet seat cover, but then she had pouted, and guilelessly rubbed at the bump on the back of her head, and yes, he probably did some breast-ogling while she huffed and puffed, but in the end, there was nothing that he could deny her.

As he carried the bags out to the car, he noted the satisfied smile on her face. "You did all this on purpose?"

Her blue eyes were all innocence. "You said that you needed decorations. I was only trying to help."

"Get out. You were trying to humiliate me in front of the good citizens of this town."

"Did it work?"

"Not saying, in case you decide that I haven't been tormented enough."

Send For
2 FREE BOOKS
Today!

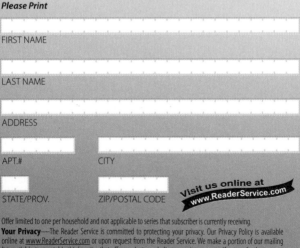

I accept your offer!

Please send me two free
Harlequin® Blaze® novels and
two mystery gifts (gifts worth
about $10). I understand that
these books are completely
free—even the shipping and
handling will be paid—and I am
under no obligation to purchase
anything, ever, as explained on the
back of this card.

151/351 HDL FNN5

Please Print

FIRST NAME

LAST NAME

ADDRESS

APT.#   CITY

STATE/PROV.   ZIP/POSTAL CODE

Visit us online at
www.ReaderService.com

Then she snickered, that same smoky laugh, and he found himself smiling, even while carrying a Santa toilet seat cover.

No one was at the corps building to witness the great unloading of joyeux de crap. Chloe studied each room of the building, the TV room, the kitchen, the bunkrooms and the lawn, making decisions about what should go where. The Christmas tree needed to go against the bay window in the TV room. There were ornaments in gold and silver, and while in the store, he'd thought they were ugly. Here, against the butt-ugly white walls, they looked...nice.

"What do you think?" she asked, sounding like a kid in a candy store.

"Not so bad," he admitted, plucking a jingle bell hair ornament out of the bag. He wanted to see it in her hair, see the shadows reflected in the golden bells. He held it out, waiting for her to take it.

She didn't move.

Eric took a step closer, the scent of pine and cinnamon filling his nose. His fingers inched forward, more than a little desperation in the movement. Take it, he urged silently, but still, she didn't move, only watched him with that shimmering blue gaze, daring him to touch her. Daring him to touch the untouchable Chloe.

Slowly he placed the band in her hair, pushing the hair away from her eyes, feeling the silk strands skim over his hand like a dream. And still she watched him. Soft red lips fell open, an invitation, a tease.

Twelve years ago he had kissed those lips under the mistletoe at the Price Mansion. Unable to resist, Eric lowered his head...

Just as a ray of sunlight caught the gold on her hand.

Taking a shaky step back, Eric grabbed the first ornament he could find, the dancing penguins, and skewered them to the tree. He made a mess of the position, and smart Chloe didn't

try to fix it, didn't try to come near him. Instead she pulled
the band from her hair, and watched him safely from afar.

Eric told himself that it was for the best.

FOR THE REST of the day, she was much more cautious. There
was a hunger inside her that ached when she got too near Eric.
She wanted to believe it was the remains of her injuries, but
she knew that wasn't the truth. Every time he was close, she
could see the dark gold stubble on the hard line of his jaw.
The long muscles in his back rippled as he adjusted the lights
on the roof. Her eyes drifted lower, watching his thighs flex,
watching the way the soft denim hugged the two perfectly
molded curves of his Grade-A butt. She made him move the
lights lower two inches, just so she could watch him.

Watching was so much smarter than touching, she reminded herself.

He was careful, too.

In the small kitchen, when he'd cooked two quesadillas
for lunch, he had stayed close to the stove, hovering dangerously near the gas flames rather than venturing dangerously
near her.

As he climbed down from the ladder, he loaded the re-
maining lights into a box, never looking at her, never talking
to her, never touching her.

She followed him into the building, twisting the gold band
on her hand.

Yes, it was definitely safer that way.

"I SHOULD TAKE you to the house. You're probably tired."

The digital clock on the wall said it was nearly seven
o'clock, but she didn't feel tired. She felt curiously buzzed.

"I would like to get cleaned up." She had barely broken a
sweat—Eric had done all the work today—but she had to say
something to fill the space between them.

The somber gray gaze drifted over her face, over her chest, and she could feel her breasts tighten and swell. He didn't say a word.

The car ride was quiet and uneventful. He drove up a long hill, away from the lights of the town, parking the car in front of a small stone cottage. Not exactly what she had been expecting. He looked more the modern contemporary condo type, but this place…it was perfect.

Inside, the rooms were decorated in earthy greens and yellows and browns, accented with huge splashes of color in the modern paintings on the walls. It was a tasteful design job, the very sort of non-monied look that only real money can buy.

The only thing missing was any trace of Christmas. There was no tree, no garlands, no Santas, no…nothing.

"Very nice," she murmured. "Too busy to decorate your own place, huh?"

He met her eyes evenly and shrugged. "Why? You do the work and then later you undo all the work you've done. Seems like a waste of time to me."

She managed a half smile because there was no point in arguing with a holiday dilettante. "Okay."

"You have issues with that?" he pressed, obviously willing to waste time arguing with her, so there was hope for the man yet.

"Life is a waste of time. You're born, and then at some point in the future, you die. And yet we don't all roll over like dogs and give up."

Okay, it was harsher than she intended, but this whole bah-humbug attitude was a cop-out.

"You think I'm a coward because I don't decorate my house for the holidays?"

She crossed her arms, tilted her head and stared him down. "Yes."

She thought he was going to argue again, but instead he

ducked away. "Shower's in the back. Towels in plain sight. Not Christmas towels, mind you, but they're effective."

"Pfftttt," she grumbled, just loud enough that he could hear and then turned to get clean.

The bathroom was a dark royal blue with rich tile work in emerald green and white. A smattering of maroon and Christmas gold would have blended nicely and she considered whipping up a nice little bow and basket with a few jewel-toned ornaments thrown in for good measure. She wondered if he would get angry, and decided it would be good for him to have his very orderly world shaken up.

The man needed some excitement, she told herself, stripping off her clothes, catching sight of her naked body in the mirror. It always surprised her to see that face looking back. To see the sexy curves, ripe and decadent. It thrilled her, made her feel…alive. After a few minutes she dragged her eyes away, embarrassed by her own ego. Instead she focused on the bathroom, beautiful jewel tones, and yet there was no soul in this place.

Everything in this bathroom was pristine and untouched, and it cried out to be humanized. Even the glass shelves on the wall were bare. Doing nothing but gathering dust. She climbed up on the toilet seat, washcloth in hand, prepared to test her theory, and a bottle of air freshener fell to the floor. A polite knock sounded at the door.

"Yes?" she called out, putting the bottle back in place. The door opened, and she hid her smile before she pivoted to face him.

He was eyes to her breasts, and that delicious gray gaze darkened to sin. Since he was a medic, she knew it wasn't anything he hadn't seen before, but yeah, her ego got a little stroke.

"I heard the crash."

"Oops. Sorry about that."

He swallowed, frowned, then looked up at the shelves. "What were you doing up there?"

"Dusting." She presented the formerly clean cloth to him. He didn't focus on the dirt, only on the sight of her bare breasts. Enjoying the moment, she stepped into the shower, leaving the glass door ajar, and let the water run down her face, her chest.

It was hedonistic and shameless. She was flaunting herself, flaunting her sexuality, and she wondered if she'd always been like this. Maybe she was a nudist. Maybe she was a stripper. Both would explain this need to show her skin, but not everything. Not the way her breath caught when he looked at her. Not the way she ached to have him touch her. She reached up and adjusted the spray, making sure that the water pulsed over her, just so. Maybe she was a porn star, she thought, giving him her best come-hither glance.

Eric shut the shower door.

Maybe not a porn star.

"So you're staying, then?" she called out, adding shampoo to her hair, savoring the rich scent of coconut and the ripe scent of danger. He didn't say anything, but he didn't run away, either.

The soap was citrus, a tart scent that tickled her nose, and she lathered all over, washing her arms, her breasts, ridding herself of the antiseptic hospital smell, reveling in the heady smells of nature. "Love the soap," she told him, raising one leg, marveling at her own toned thighs and calves. This body felt new, powerful, like a well-honed blade. Beautiful, yet lethal.

From the other side of the glass, she could see him watching her. The heat of the water was no match for the heat in the air, and she wanted him to notice her, to want her. She didn't know why this feeling was so strong, but it was there, driving her forward to put on the show of her life. And the fast beat of her pulse told her that she wasn't accustomed to men watching her. She wasn't accustomed to *letting* men watch her. She knew that, but all this power was too exhilarating. And too new.

Her hands ran between her thighs, using the soap in novel and exhilarating ways.

"You shouldn't do that."

His words surprised her, breaking through the steamy confines.

"You don't have to watch," she reminded him, then began humming to herself.

Eric stayed silent, defeated by logic, and she smiled. Back against the tile, she let the water run through her hair, washing away the bubbles and the grime, washing away a whole other life. It felt like a new beginning, a chance to start over. To finally have all the things that she'd ever wanted.

"You're married."

The words hit her like a slap of cold water. She wrenched off the faucet, threw open the door. "There has been no touching, no kissing. I've done nothing wrong. Neither have you."

Eric didn't look convinced, but then again, he was still there, his gaze skimming over her, warming her skin. She stood before him, heart pounding in her chest. Excitement, fear, sex. Hooded eyes watched her, no excitement or fear, but the sex was there. And she noticed what was missing. Surprise.

"You've seen me like this before."

"No."

She couldn't shake the feeling he was lying to her. The intimacy between them sparked memories inside her. Dreamy memories, but she thought they were more than just a dream.

"You've touched me before," she whispered, not as sure as she'd intended. She wanted to understand what was real in her mind, what was only a dream.

For a long while, he stayed frozen, but then he nodded. Once.

"Did you touch me here?" she asked, running light fingertips over her stimulated nipples, hearing him suck in his breath. She tweaked one rosy peak, staring up at him, chasing after the dream, wanting so badly to know the truth between them. "Did I like it?"

He didn't answer, not that she expected him to, so she continued. "I bet you weren't easy, were you? I think I would like that, the pain." It was like talking to a wall. A wall with a heartbeat so loud that she could hear it, or maybe that was only her own feeble heart.

"But you did hurt me, didn't you?" A crystal drop of water caught his gaze, and her fingertips followed, chasing it down her torso, below her slim belly where it quivered and hung.

His eyes fell to her fingers. "Yes."

It wasn't what she wanted to hear. A lie was so much easier. Since the accident, she had felt so powerful, so desirable, as if she could have any man in the world. But she wasn't that woman, and he wasn't that man. And now she felt like she'd come home from a party at two in the morning, with thick thighs, blurry makeup and an empty hole where a soul was supposed to be.

Her perfect body shone in the mirror. No thick thighs, no blurry makeup and the hole was just as real. She wanted to wrap herself in a towel, wanted to run and wanted to hide, but she wasn't going to give him that.

Instead, she gave him a cold smile. "That's why I want to hate you, why I want to make you hurt. You hurt me."

The dark gaze lifted to hers, and she saw sadness there, regret mixed with desire. "You remember?"

She closed her eyes, tried to break though the fog and the steamy dreams, but she couldn't remember anything beyond the urgency in his face. She could only feel his mouth against her neck. Hesitant. Unsure.

It all felt so real.

Her eyes flew open, expecting to find his mouth on her skin, but he was standing where he had been before. Unmoving. It wasn't supposed to be like this at Christmas. It was supposed to be happy and magical. They were supposed to kiss under the mistletoe and he was going to love her forever.

Everything twisted inside her, and she hated that she was naked. Perfect. Naked. And still ashamed.

"Of course I remember," she lied, and then decided that today he was going to hurt just as badly as she had hurt before. The mirror called her, and she twirled around, angry, aroused, but mostly wanting to make him pay. For what, she had no idea.

HIS CHEST FELT as if it was about to explode. Her eyes flickered with anger at him, all deserved. And yet she still stood there, reflected in the glass. Naked, wet, gorgeous, like some fantasy, but this one was real.

Every inch of him, every white-hot hardened inch of him wanted to touch her. Wanted to reach out and stroke the glistening flesh, wanted to see if she was wet all over.

But he didn't, because she had been right. Eric Marshall was a coward. Her legs parted, and her left hand, currently ringless, drew small, lazy circles on the inside of her thigh. His gaze followed her finger, tracking the circles until he was dizzy from those small, easy movements.

It was Chloe, and yet not Chloe. The bravado and the boldness were all still there, but the vulnerability and the shame were gone. This was a woman baptized in fire, and she was determined to drag him into the flames as well.

Eric stood frozen because it was nothing that he didn't deserve.

"I couldn't do this for you before," she whispered, but he couldn't take his eyes from her hand, from the swollen bare skin between her legs. She'd had dark hair there before, untrimmed, unpolished. It had been soft. And wet.

Her middle finger slid between the two swollen lips and he could see the damp, see the pearly sheen of moisture on her. He heard a sound, a growl. She looked up at his pained face in the mirror and smiled. It wasn't an invitation. This was the smile of a woman who had his balls in the palm of her hand.

Her finger disappeared inside her. He watched her hips move to accept the intrusion, and he felt his shaft grow, just as she intended.

"Chloe," he heard himself whisper.

She met his eyes, smiled, feeling a spark of recognition. Chloe. She was Chloe. "I like my name on your tongue."

Instantly he licked his lips, mouth dry, parched, aching.

"I have to leave."

Her sigh stretched out to hell and back. "Is it so easy to leave me?"

"No."

"Do you remember when we were together?" she asked. Her eyes closed, her hips moving to her own private rhythm.

"I remember."

"Why do I hate you?" she asked, her voice desperate and pleading and instantly he saw the trick.

"I thought you remembered."

"A few hazy things. Not much. Not enough." Her eyes were sad as she wrapped the towel around her perfect body. "I wanted you to hurt like I did. I wanted your heart to ache like mine. But it's not your heart, only your cock. It's not enough," she announced, and Eric watched as Chloe left the room, leaving his aching cock, his aching conscience, his aching heart behind.

4

THEY REACHED AN unspoken agreement that night. Chloe kept her clothes on, and Eric kept his thoughts to himself. Chloe.

Chloe Skidmore. She had remembered her name when he said it. The sound was so familiar to her. She wondered what her married name was. She wondered about her husband.

"I'd like to use your computer," she said politely, after dinner was done, after the strains of Beethoven were playing softly through the room.

"There's no record of your marriage."

She was surprised that he had looked. Surprised that he cared. "Maybe you were looking in the wrong places."

"And you know the right places?" He raised one brow in the manor-born style designed to quash any question like a bug. The Marshall family had mastered the supercilious brow. His father, Edwin Marshall. His mother, Tinsley. Their only son, Eric.

"How are your parents?" she asked, deciding to change the subject.

"Old, bitter, rich."

She smiled at the thought.

"You remember them?"

Oh, yes, she remembered them. She disliked them both. The Marshall family, the Price family, all the families that lived in the hills of Pine Crest. Sure, the Skidmores had lived in a mansion, but they didn't belong there. She remembered that as well.

Her nod was jerky and tight, as was the lock in his jaw.

They were two sides of the same coin. If the fates flipped heads, your life was awesome. Tails, then you kept flipping the coin over and over again, trying to not be tails.

"Why are you a paramedic?" It was a noble profession, an honorable profession, but not exactly a silver-spoon sort of job. She'd figured that he would have been a lawyer. Harvard or Yale. Maybe Stanford if he'd developed a wild hair. Of course, Eric had always had a wild hair.

For the first time, his gaze seemed familiar to her. Rebellious, a little bit defiant and nervous, all at the same time. "I hated law school."

"Yale?" she asked. Edwin Marshall was a third-generation graduate.

"Stanford."

Chloe laughed. "I bet Daddy was horrified."

"It was either that or William and Mary."

A state school. "Quelle horreur."

"Did you ever go to school? You always bragged that you were going to NYU."

Memories swirled like wispy figments, flitting through her brain, just out of reach. Some things were so clear. Some things, like leaving her home and venturing out into the world of college or men or making money, were still a big ol' question mark.

"Graduated top of the class, with a degree in finance," she lied in grand Chloe Skidmore style.

"And after that?"

She lifted her shoulders in a casual shrug.

He was watching her, studying her and something akin to sympathy entered his eyes. "It'll come back. You suffered a blow to the head, on top of the trauma of the fire. It's pretty common, actually."

And she was back to feeling the victim. She hated that feeling, hated the idea that she was dependent on him. Hated even more that all she had to do was leave. But she couldn't. No, that was the hardest truth of all.

Needing something to distract her, she looked around the comfortable room, instantly noticing what was absent.

The bay window overlooked a lit-up view of the town, glowing in green and red lights. The walls held an assortment of art. Splashy Dali painting, noir Edward Hopper and a traditional Monet. The bookshelves held a mix of new and old. Fiction and non. This was a man who had created a welcoming home, and yet…

"Why don't you have a Christmas tree?" she asked, because there was a spot near the window. A perfect spot. Made to hold a welcoming tree. She wanted her Christmas. She wanted her holiday.

"For one person? Seems like overkill to me."

"You say overkill, I say heresy. Let's cut one down. Do they still have the forest of firs on the back ridge?"

His eyes narrowed. "How much do you remember?"

"How much should I remember?" she asked, holding his gaze for a moment, searching for a past. Eventually it was Eric who looked away.

"Let's go kill a tree," he answered, and she was glad that she wasn't the only one who couldn't walk away. Then she looked down at her ringless left hand, and waited for some feeling of guilt. But instead the woman with a hole in her soul felt nothing at all, except a brief flicker of happiness when

Eric helped her into her coat, his hands lingering through layers of material.

It wasn't the touch that she had longed for, but for tonight, it was enough.

THE NIGHT AIR was cold, with the sort of wind that put a burn on your cheeks. From the top of the ridge, a whole forest of pine trees stood, a line of defense that had separated the town of Pine Crest from the world for hundreds of years. The town was full of lines and boundaries. Walls that weren't meant to be scaled. Mountains that weren't meant to be climbed. Chloe remembered being up here before, sneaking through the barbed-wired fence with a large group of kids. That night, she had been out of breath, wearing the ugly moth-eaten wool coat. When she was growing up, she'd always hated her clothes, the big tent dresses, the ill-fitting jeans.

Instinctively her hands skimmed over her hips, checking the shape, relieved to realize that no, she was skinny. Chloe the Cow was no more.

Chloe the Cow.

She had gone home in tears that night. Not in front of the others, because Chloe would never let anyone know that the words got to her. But somewhere between the end of the mountain trail and where the town sidewalk began, the tears had started to flow.

Chloe was a great secret crier. Her father hadn't liked it when she cried. Her parents had divorced when she was four, Betsy Skidmore leaving Pine Crest behind and eventually finding her way to Arkansas, where she remarried, had four other sons and left Buddy and Chloe Skidmore in the dust.

Eric had caught up with her on the sidewalk that night, falling into step beside her, not saying a word, until eventually the tears stopped falling. He'd been wearing a leather bomber jacket with the fleece collar pulled up around his neck. He hadn't worn a hat because Eric never wore a hat, and there was snow in his hair, making him look older, more like a man.

He had walked her to the edge of the mansion, his hands jammed in his pockets. "You know we were just kidding."

As apologies went, it wasn't the best, but he was Eric Marshall, and he was tall and serious and had clothes that she would have killed for. He wasn't exactly nice to her, but Chloe was a girl and there were things that she understood. When he was with his friends, she wouldn't be acknowledged. But when he was alone...

Eric Marshall wanted her.

Her sixteen-year-old heart understood that. Even with the mountain of a coat, even with the extra forty pounds. It was a heady feeling for a fat girl from the wrong side of town.

He was Eric Marshall.

She had kissed him for the first time that night. Oh, no, Eric would never had touched her on his own, she knew that then. But when she had reached up, and pulled his head down, she remembered his arms locking around her, locking them together.

He smelled of Halston and money and lust, but his kiss had been everything that a first kiss should have been. Urgent yet respectful, passionate yet tender. His touch had been careful, never out of bounds, never going too far. No, Eric Marshall never went too far.

Not that night, anyway.

Yes, she managed to suppress the moonstruck sigh, but Chloe couldn't keep from touching a finger to her mouth. Not twenty feet away, Eric was attacking a tree trunk with heavy swings of an ax. His parka was thrown carelessly in the snow, and each time he pulled back to swing, Chloe could see the raw power in his shoulders, the bunch of muscles underneath the wool shirt. There was something very...stimulating about the sight of a man performing manual labor. The mouth that had kissed her so long ago was pulled tight, muttering what looked to be swear words, but she didn't mind.

"How's it going?" she yelled, mainly to be cheery and perky, and all those things that Chloe Skidmore had never been in the past.

Eric stopped in mid-swing and glared.

"You know we don't have to do this," she told him, almost feeling guilty, but not quite.

"Yes, we do."

"Not on my account."

He pushed the ax into the ground. "You wanted a tree."

"Not if you're going to be grumpy about it."

"This isn't grumpy."

And no, this wasn't grumpy Eric. He'd never been one of those happy-go-lucky types. She remembered that much. His complaints about the high school science teacher, Mr.... Crown. Yes, Mr. Crown. The general dislike of all things football, especially the Redskins, and the way he vowed to one day trash his father's car. Except he never had. No, Eric had always been too smart for that.

"Thank you," she said simply.

"For what?"

"For cutting the tree."

He shrugged carelessly, as if it didn't mean anything, but that was another thing she remembered about Eric Marshall. He never did anything that he didn't want to do. Even cutting a tree.

Or kissing a girl.

The moonlight touched down on his hair, and she sighed happily, touching her lips, and remembering a little bit more.

THE TREE WAS two feet taller than the ceiling, and had to get a haircut. Chloe supervised, and Eric tried his damnedest to trim the branches, but every time he cut, Chloe was back at him to repair the damage.

"No, that looks awful. Whack off that little bit that's hanging to the left."

Eric looked down from the ladder to where Chloe was calling orders like a general. A very sexy general, with a great chest, which, when he closed his eyes, he could remember in exquisite detail, but a general nonetheless. He blocked out the Chloe-naked vision and grabbed the edge of a long, fluffy branch. "This one?"

She shook her head, and pointed. "Above."

He climbed up a step. "Here?"

She motioned him to the left. "Over six inches."

He reached out, shook hands with the tree. "Here?" When he glanced down, she was smiling like the devil. "If you don't play nice, I'm forfeiting my Christmas elf duties."

"But you make such a cute elf," she teased, her voice wrapping around him like the best Christmas present ever.

And yes, he was hard again. "I'm up here for five minutes more and then it's done. It'll look awesome, and you will take great pleasure in telling me how great a job I've done. We got a deal?"

Chloe cocked her head, and he was happy to see some of the fight back in her eyes. "I don't remember you being so insecure."

He didn't want to tell her it wasn't insecurity, but the painful hard-on that he was lugging around like a lead balloon. "I like women to pander to my ego. It makes me feel like an unevolved man. Now can we finish the goddamn tree?"

She folded her arms across her chest. He noticed. "Cranky, aren't we?"

He trimmed the last bits of the branch, and oops, some of it might have fallen into her hair. Quickly he climbed down the ladder, and was going to walk away, but she stood there, watching him with happy eyes, and his feet decided to stay.

"You have a branch in your hair," he told her, just like an idiot, and he reached out, pushing his hand through the dark cloud, wondering if it was a sin to debranch a married woman. He didn't think so, and so he continued to stroke the soft strands, his fingers tangling somewhere they had no business tangling.

His brain formed words, words reminding her about the ring on her hand, words that explained in great detail why she needed to move a step back. Why she needed to stay away from him.

The words never came. Her mouth opened and closed, and he watched the tiny flutter in her throat. The center of her eyes grew dark and wide, like an ever-expanding night sky, sucking in everything in its path. He was trapped in her gaze, mesmerized by his own reflection in the heavens.

He didn't want to kiss her, he didn't want to covet another man's wife, but the smell of pine trees and Chloe took him back to another place, another time, and he wanted so badly to relive the past and show her that he was that epic man reflected in her eyes. He covered the lush mouth, feeling the hungry press of her lips, and his breathing stopped, his mind starting to spin and whir as the lack of oxygen kicked in, as the pure power of her kiss bolted through his mouth, his body, his brain.

Before she had kissed him like a young girl, innocent, eager, passionate, uncaring, but tonight she kissed him as a woman. Wary, knowing, with an edge of desperation.

The knowledge that this wasn't going to happen again. A last kiss.

Somewhere along the way, Chloe had gotten smart.

His arms pulled her tight, his hands pushing underneath the back of her shirt, wanting to feel the warmth of Chloe, wanting to feel the softness of Chloe. She wasn't wearing a bra tonight, but he didn't dare explore, didn't dare touch anything more than innocent skin. There was a certain hypocrisy to that line of thinking since his tongue was capturing hers in the most non-innocent way possible, but Eric clung to his standards, meager as they were.

Her hands jammed inside the back pockets of his jeans, and she pushed his cock into the wedge of her thighs, more non-innocence, but there were barriers of clothes between them.

This was a frenzied dance of metaphorical sex, which seemed acceptable. Frustrating, yet acceptable under the tall branches of a Christmas pine. Her hips ground against him, torturing his cock. He could remember dates like this, the silent fumblings of pseudo-sex in clothes, but it had never felt so frantic, so essential.

He wanted to touch her, to dig inside her jeans, to test the softness there as well, but his hands stayed locked against the heated skin of her back. She breathed into his mouth, sucking on his tongue, and he wanted to ask her to stop, because he was about to explode, but the sensation of her lips was making speech impossible. With each stroke of her tongue, her hips, his desire consumed him and he pushed against her, tumbling them onto the floor, arms tangled, and yet all clothes intact. It was that intactness that kept him sane. Kept Eric from feeling like an ass, even as he lay on top of her, his cock nestled ever so snugly between her thighs. As if it belonged.

His eyes opened, while her own eyes were tightly closed, as if she didn't want to see who she was with. He understood that need, better than most. He had felt that way with her before, and he had the emotional scars, not to mention the bad mix tape to prove it. When he was in high school, wanting her was like a drug, and yet he'd been unwilling to deal with the realities of the social order.

He looked down at her face, watching her as they moved.

Her breathing was labored, her glorious chest rising up and down with each stroke of his hips. Taut legs wrapped around him, binding them together even more tightly, but there were so many things wrong with this picture.

He wanted her to open her eyes. To see him. To acknowledge him. To know who was there, but he couldn't ask for that. Asking was wrong, and his ego would live, so he satisfied himself with watching the dark shadow of lashes against her pale skin, amazed at how much she was still the same Chloe of before. The same Chloe Skidmore who had teased his cock more than any other woman alive. And yet she never knew, because Eric excelled at hiding the truth from people. His family, his friends, Chloe, himself. He thrust faster, angry at her, angry at the man she married, angry at himself, angry at the whole damn world. It felt so good to give in to the anger, to press hard, hard, harder…

Then she gasped, and her eyes flew open, and he could see the helplessness there. The same need he'd seen on the night of the fire, asking him for things that he was more than happy to give. He remembered seeing the flare of pain, quickly replaced by lust. Blind lust. The words almost made him laugh, but he could feel the tightening in his muscles, his cock full, and he pushed again, once, twice…

This time her hips rose, hung suspended like a bridge against him, and time stopped. His orgasm came, spilling into his jeans, a cold uncomfortable dampness that reminded him that he wasn't thirteen anymore, that he was a responsible, grown-up man. Eric jumped up, his mind still a jumble of mush, and held out a hand to Chloe. She looked at him, with a confused and sated gaze that only made him want her more.

No. No. No.

"We can't do this again," he stated in an extra firm voice. It was his authority voice, used to calm frightened kids and drunk trauma vics.

"Technically, we didn't—" she held up quote fingers "—do anything."

"Don't split hairs, honey. Wrong is wrong. You just give me stupid brain and I want to forget important things. Like you were in the hospital two days ago. Like I promised not to do this. Like you're married."

As he spoke, he could see the fog of sex clearing from her eyes, only to be replaced by something else. Anger. "Stupid brain? I give you stupid brain? Way to pump up my ego, Romeo."

And out of everything he said, that was the thing she picked out? Eric pushed a hand through his hair. Chloe mad at him was better than Chloe not anything at him. It was safer. There would be no possibility of sex if she hated him—or technically if she remembered the fact that she already hated him. So that was the strategy that Eric went with; dumb, yes, but effective. "Put a woman with a great set of…" He tried to think insulting, degrading, sexist. Unfortunately, the Marshall family had strong standards about behavior with women, and polite sensibilities. "*Bosoms* under my nose, and man is like this giant magnet that follows a female, seeking out…" Oh, God. This was harder than he'd thought. "You know," he finished, flailing a descriptive hand.

"You know? You mean sex, Eric? You mean screwing?"

He nodded. "Yes, that's what I mean."

"And any woman with a set of *bosoms* gives you stupid brain?"

He could see where this was going. He knew what Chloe wanted him to say. That it was Chloe that he wanted. Only Chloe. Even madder than hell, she still wanted him to admit what he had never admitted to her. Not once.

Then he stared into her eyes, and realized that this was the same vulnerable girl he had known forever. Sure, the shell had changed, but inside, her heart was still made of glass.

He should break it. Throw it down on the ground, stomp on it because…

She was married.

Eric opened his mouth.

"Not every woman, Chloe. Never every woman. Only you."

5

THEY WERE WORDS she'd wanted to hear forever. Or at least it felt like forever. Chloe slumped onto the couch because her knees didn't feel so good.

Eric wanted her.

It should have thrilled her. It should have pandered to an already bruised ego, and for a second it did. She looked down at her left hand, at the heavy band of gold on her finger.

"I don't feel married." She sounded like a brat, like a kid who can't get what they want. She hated that she sounded that way. She wanted to be brave and strong, with principles and moral turpitude, but instead, all she could do was hate the heavy circular padlock that she wore on her hand. The ring wasn't even pretty. It was plain, with no personality, no engraving, no sense of style. It wasn't a piece of jewelry that she would have ever picked out.

"But you are married," Eric said. He sat on the other end of the couch, not close, but his voice was nice, soothing, not at all disapproving that she sounded like a brat. She appreciated that.

"I've been trying to remember a name. A face. A date. A house. Something, but it's all blank."

"Maybe you're trying for the wrong things. How does he make you feel? Happy, sad? Afraid?"

"Right now I'm mad, but I think that's frustration, and I can't very well blame him for that, now can I?" She tried to laugh. Failed.

"Maybe you're blocking something out. Why did you end up at the mansion that night?"

"It's home."

"But why did you run, Chloe? Did you ever think about that? Maybe you were running away. Coming home. Maybe because you're afraid of him."

It would have been easy if her husband were some vile piece of trash, but Chloe thought she would have remembered that. Sadly she shook her head. "I wouldn't have married a man unless I loved him."

"So what sort of man would you have married?" He threw an arm over the back of the couch, a comfortable gesture only belied by the intensity of his voice.

She traced the line of the blue stripes on the couch with a slow finger, pretending to think about the question, but the answers were so easy. "A kind man. Strong. Not stupid."

Things were different between them now. Before she had wanted to touch him, to shock him into seeing what was between them. But now, they both knew what was between them.

She didn't dare touch him anymore, because if she did, she didn't think she could stop. And although Chloe Skidmore suspected she was a woman who could live with those sorts of muddled principles, she didn't think Eric could.

It was why she loved him.

"Funny or serious?"

She smiled, and glanced up. "Serious."

He looked at her, surprised. "Not funny?"

"Funny is good, but funny is fleeting. Serious stays forever." She remembered the day she failed her English test. Mr.

Landry had hated her because she liked to talk in class. She'd made a thirty-seven, which she didn't deserve because she'd written a really good essay, but Landry wanted to teach her a lesson about respect. Eric had been there after class, telling her that it didn't matter. Everyone else had laughed it off, but not Eric. He understood.

"What about looks? Dark or blond?"

"Dark," she answered instantly.

"Facial hair? Beards are very popular. Maybe a goatee."

"Hate facial hair," she answered firmly. "Brown hair. No beard. No mustache."

"Bulked up? Skinny?"

Chloe thought for a minute. "Not skinny. Not big. There was one guy I dated in…" *D.C. Oh, God. She had lived in Baltimore. In an apartment. With a sewing machine and two shelves of African violets. One plant had been losing leaves, and she'd been worried. Not "they'd been worried." She had been worried.*

She twisted at the gold band.

"Where?" he prodded.

"I don't know. It was almost there," she lied, "but then it disappeared."

"Do you remember the guy? Were you scared of the guy? Maybe he had a temper?"

It was such a strange question. "Why are you so fixated on the scary dude?"

He laughed a fake laugh. "Wishful thinking."

"Gee, thanks."

"Sorry."

She sat there on the couch, separated by a tiny gold band and two feet of empty air, and indulged a long moment of self-pity. "What are we going to do?"

"Wait."

Her heart stopped for a moment, hope filling places it didn't know better. "Wait for what?"

"You'll get the last pieces of your memory back, Chloe. You're almost there. And when you remember everything…" His voice trailed off.

"What?"

"Then you go home."

Home. So why did this feel like home? "I don't want to go home."

Eric hesitated for a long second. "I don't want you to," he said, his voice husky.

"Thank you."

"For what?"

"For taking me in. For saying things you didn't want to say. It means a lot."

He wanted to tell her things, he felt the words on his tongue, but just as his mouth was about to say them, the doorbell rang.

It was his dad.

"Hello, Eric. Aren't you going to let me in?"

Eric stayed in the doorway, silently yelling at himself for not changing his jeans. But no, he had to sit there next to Chloe, sharing the same oxygen, trying to win some bonus points for being nice. If there was a God, his father wouldn't see through the heavy wooden door to the stains on his pants.

It was a low point in his life.

"I'm busy at the moment, Dad. Can we talk later? I'll call you."

"I heard you had company."

Hell. "I know that it seems crazy to you, but I do have friends. Two."

"I heard she was female."

"This isn't a good time, Dad. I have a tree to decorate,

presents to wrap. In fact, that's what I was doing. Wrapping your present. That's why you can't come in."

Edwin Marshall didn't look convinced. Sadly, Edwin Marshall wasn't stupid. "Women will always want you for the Marshall name, for the money, for the family jewels. Be careful."

Red-hot anger pulsed through Eric's already overheated body. His normally calm blood pressure shot up to at least one-fifty, and that wasn't even counting the damp state of his privates.

Eric flung open the door. "Yeah, maybe that's why Mom married you, for the money, for the name, for the jewels, but I'm not you, Dad. Don't want to be, and I don't need to wrap your present. It's a gift certificate. From an electronics store. Two hundred bucks, which is more than I wanted to spend, more than you deserve, but I'm a decent human being, and really couldn't care less about the Marshall money."

"You would have made a great lawyer."

"Go away, Dad. I'm having sex. With a female. She doesn't care about the money, either, and the only family jewels she's interested in are mine."

With that, he slammed the door shut in his father's face.

Stupid, yes, but goddamn satisfying.

And the best part was the look on Chloe's face.

A LOSS FOR WORDS was a condition that Chloe rarely suffered from, and she recovered quicker than she would have expected. And there was Eric, chest heaving, as if he'd just run a marathon, or just shocked his father, which was probably just as exhausting. "You shouldn't have said that."

He didn't look like a man who could give his father a coronary. Of course, he was an EMT, so maybe that wasn't a concern. Still, Chloe was concerned. Yes, his parents were awful, but they were family, and that she understood. You stood by family, accepting the good and the bad, and if you didn't, you ran away to Arkansas, leaving behind the very people who cared.

"Are you after my money?" he asked, a small smile twitching at the corners of his mouth.

"No."

He returned to the couch.

"You told him we were…" Once again she was at a loss for words.

"Having sex?"

"We weren't having sex."

"Maybe not in the clinical sense of the word, but what would you call it, Chloe?"

"Making love," she said quietly.

The smile disappeared, and he pushed a hand through his hair. "I'm sorry."

"For what?"

"For my father. For me. For earlier. You should leave, Chloe. This isn't right."

No, it wasn't right, but she had stopped caring, and she wondered if this was how Betsy Skidmore had felt, how she had left her family behind. Right at this moment, Chloe was tired of fighting. Only she was sure about one thing. Eric Marshall. She came and stood before him, not really sure about the future, not sure there was a future. Not sure if she had a family somewhere, not sure if Eric's parents would ever speak to him again. There were too many things to worry about, but not right now.

Now was the time for the truth. "I love you. I have always loved you. Not your family, no, but you, yes."

He didn't smile, didn't grin, only scowled as if she'd given him some nasty disease. "Chloe, go away."

Except that she didn't. She could read the panic in his face, and knew that she'd finally said the perfect thing. "Go away because you don't want me?"

"Because I do."

She folded her arms across her chest, feeling right at home. It was a wonderful feeling, standing under the mistletoe with the Christmas tree blinking merrily. No, this was where she belonged. "If you want me, that's all the more reason to stay."

"That's the concussion talking."

"That's my heart talking. Possibly my ladyparts as well, but I'm okay with that. It's what's right."

Stubbornly he shook his head.

Boldly she put a hand on his zipper. He was hard. Smelled of sex. He was toast.

"Can we deal with tomorrow tomorrow? I want my happy now. Maybe that's why I can't remember. Because I don't want to remember."

"And when it all comes back?"

"Can we deal with that tomorrow, too?" She pulled her shirt over her head, warmed by the fire in his eyes, panic turning to resignation, because they belonged together. At least for now.

"I can't walk away from you," he warned, giving her one last chance to be smart.

"Then don't," she said simply and walked into his arms, and this time he didn't walk away.

THEY TUMBLED ONTO the floor beneath the mistletoe. When Chloe looked up and saw the sprig, she giggled, but then stopped giggling when Eric's mouth suckled her breast.

The pain was exquisite, like lightning tipped with gold, but she didn't care that he was hurting her. The pleasure was too great.

Her hands pushed under his shirt, and locked onto the hot skin. Her fingers explored the tight muscles, feeling the blood pump beneath his skin, hearing the catch in his breath when she touched him. For so long she had wanted this. Wanted him.

With urgent hands, he pulled away her jeans, his fingers slipping inside her.

"You were killing me. I wanted to touch you like that. Like this." She cried out at the touch. She was made for his hands, for his fingers, for his mouth.

He rose over her, and his eyes glinted jewel bright. All the casualness was gone, all the walls were down, and her heart began to race, because in this, they were one.

His mouth crashed down on hers, rough and greedy, and she reveled in the swarm of sensations. His tongue in her mouth, his finger stroking inside her. Skin to skin, heat to heat.

Needing to touch him, needing to bare him, she pulled at his jeans, getting them halfway down.

He hissed, and she rocked against him. Each time she moved, his fingers stroked her faster, more urgently, but she wanted more.

She freed him from his briefs, the velvet steel hot in her hand. He froze, met her eyes. "Not yet. Not now. This. It's for you, Chloe. Only for you."

Gently he pushed her onto her back, his fingers lightly stroking over her skin, across her arms, her neck, down her breasts. Slowly he circled the tip of each one, whispering words to her. Beautiful, golden words, and she closed her eyes, giving herself up to the dream. His lips, his hands, they touched everywhere, teasing her, seducing her. He parted her thighs, stroking her again, but slowly, easily, as if they had all the time in the world.

Chloe sighed, her thighs falling apart just as easily. She felt his mouth on her, his tongue tasting her, feasting on her. Her fingers dug into the carpet to keep her hips on the ground. Her teeth bit her lip, to keep the scream in her mouth. But then he sucked harder, greedy, so greedy, and she tasted blood.

Tiny moans broke free, gurgles of nonsense sounds and her hands beat against the floor. He laughed. He laughed, and then continued dragging her closer to the place where insanity and desire mingled. Where past and present merged. She kept reaching for more, but he wouldn't let her, reducing her to a quivering thing, begging, pleading for this.

Pleading for him.

She heard the rip of foil, the rustle of latex, and her mind registered the fact. She was falling apart, and he could still think. Could still breathe. Could still be sensible, and it made her angry.

When she felt him brush against her, she rolled on top of him, pinning him there. His eyes were surprised, pleased, and she rose up above him, the V of her thighs flicking over the head of his cock. Teasing and taunting, power running through her veins like dragonfire.

Slowly she lowered herself on him, her body stretching, swelling to accommodate him. Their eyes met and locked, and then together they began to move.

Moonlight drifted in through the window, bathing them in silvery light, and she knew that this was a Christmas that she could never forget.

Chloe Skidmore and Eric Marshall together.

6

CHLOE STRETCHED on the scrumptious bed, her fingers playing with the smooth cotton sheets, the thick duvet, the man-size pillows. She could hear the sound of the shower, Eric singing to himself. And she liked that she could make him sing in the shower, and she closed her eyes, imagining him there, naked, and wet, and waiting for her.

His body had changed after all these years. The shoulders were thick, there was a long ragged scar on his left thigh. His legs were long and lean, covered in crisp, dark hair. His chest was bigger, broader, but his hair was still as soft. She remembered playing with his hair, remembered pressing a teasing bite on his shoulder, telling him that she loved him. Telling him...

Oh, God.

Waves of hurt exploded inside her, and the pain was so much worse than what she could have ever imagined.

She remembered.

Memories assaulted her, flooded one after another, the sight of a teenaged Eric with his friends. The hard words, the mocking looks. After their night in the wine cellar—after the night that they'd made love—and she had expected him to come to her, to stand with her, but no. Twelve years ago, he stood frozen, hands carefully lodged in his pockets. He, who had taken her virginity. No, twelve years ago he stood there in silence, carefully looking away.

Pushing the hated memories aside, she tore the sheets from the bed and threw the duvet on the floor, kicking the covers aside until there was nothing left but a bare mattress. No evidence of the night they had spent together. None. Because Chloe Skidmore wouldn't be the fool again.

While Eric sang in the shower, she cried quietly and pulled on her clothes. Once again, she had gone to his bed so easily. Such a patsy. Such a cow.

Before she left, she scanned the room, but the childish mess wasn't enough. The wound that he had ripped open needed cauterizing. It needed to burn, so she dragged the sex-stained sheet into the other room, and threw it in the great stone fireplace. It took a moment for the hot coals to ignite the material, but eventually the fire did its job. Burning the evidence, burning the pain from her head.

She had come back to Pine Crest for revenge. Returned to burn him, to embarrass him, to show Eric Marshall and the Marshall family that she had risen above them. To proudly tell everyone that she was married to a rich, D.C. lawyer. That they summered on the Cape, wintered on the Riviera. That they had a garden of peonies that bloomed in the spring.

Yeah, it was all a lie, including the ring on her hand. Oh, God.

She had gotten cold feet, unable to face him, and had run home. Not to Baltimore. To the old house that she'd grown up in. There was the fire. The memory of someone's face.

Teague. Teague Price.

The Prices. The Marshalls. And then there were the Skidmores.

Why had she ever come home? To be rejected once again?

The singing stopped. The water shut off, and Chloe grabbed

her shoes and dashed out into the chilled winter's morning. The snow was bitter cold on her bare feet, but that pain would heal. She couldn't face him. Not again, and so Chloe Skidmore ran toward the outskirts of town, once again running away from the man she loved.

Once again running away from the man who had broken her heart.

7

THE ACRID SMELL of smoke was never a good sign in a house. As an EMT, Eric knew this intuitively. The alarm system brayed, just in case he didn't know by the fire in the fireplace that his relationship with Chloe Skidmore had just gone up in flames.

There was a towel wrapped around his waist, his mouth was minty fresh, but his love life was now in the toilet. Or the fireplace, as it were.

It seemed fitting. He'd known it would happen, but he hadn't realized that it would hurt so much. For twelve years he'd been trying to make up for one huge mistake, and he'd done okay with the rest of the world, but he'd never tried to make it right with the one person he'd betrayed. And now, when Santa Claus, no less, had dumped Chloe in his life once again, he still had made a mess of it, because he'd never been brave enough to tell the world how he felt about her.

He'd never been brave enough to tell the world that he loved her. Hell, he hadn't even been brave enough to tell Chloe. That was all part of being a Marshall, he guessed. Something in the gene pool that said you weren't supposed to confess that you owned a heart.

The sheets were burned to a pile of black ash. A lump of

coal would have actually been less—well, he didn't know—maybe less, *I shared your bed, and now I want to forget the whole thing—except I can't.*

He had wanted her to hate him. He laughed, a croaking, choking sound. She was married. It was better that he would be out of her life. Using the cast-iron poker, he shuffled the ashes, tiny flames still popping up. A red-hot ember bounced to the floor, and he grabbed at it, tossing it back. It took a minute for the burn to register, and he watched, fascinated by the blistered skin. The human body was an amazing thing, designed to hurt, designed to heal. Designed to fight, designed to love.

And Eric did love her. He loved fat Chloe. He loved skinny Chloe. He loved Chloe, who didn't know who she was. He loved Chloe, who would tell the world to go to hell. Chloe, who was always so much braver than him.

But not today.

Ignoring the pain in his hand, Eric threw on his clothes, and sprinted for the door. He had no idea where she had gone, but he would find her. It was Christmas Eve, a day for miracles, and maybe, just maybe, he could create a miracle of his own.

8

HE FOUND HER in room three-twenty-seven at the Bunratty Hotel. Registered under the name of Jackie Kennedy. The incognito bit cheered him up because she could have used her married name, but she hadn't.

He knocked on the door until his knuckles were raw, but he didn't stop. She was in there. He could hear her moving around, until finally he could hear footsteps on the other side of the door.

The door didn't open, but it was her voice. "Go away."

"No."

"I'll call the police."

"You don't have any money. You can't pay for this room. People aren't happy with that."

"I have my wallet. It was here all the time."

That stopped him. Suddenly, Chloe wasn't the damsel in distress anymore. Chloe had money. A driver's license with her name on it. A telephone with her husband's number on speed dial. Chloe had a life of her own.

"I'm sorry."

"I don't care."

"I do."

She opened the door, and she was barefoot, no make-up,

her eyes were swollen and red, and she was perfect. "Why are you here?"

"To apologize." It wasn't exactly what he needed to say, but it was step one, the first of what was probably twelve, because God knows, he needed a twelve-step program to do a relationship right.

"Is that all?" Her brow lifted, because she could read his mind so well.

"No," he answered.

Blue eyes blazed with anger. Waiting. He thought that was a good sign. She could have slammed the door in his face. She could have called the police. But instead, she was waiting. For him.

"Tell me about your husband." He thought he should start there, because her marriage seemed to be the largest obstacle in the room.

She slammed the door in his face.

Obviously her husband was not the largest obstacle in the room.

From down below in the lobby, Eric could hear the carolers singing. He peered over the stairwell and saw Santa Claus watching him, smiling, like some secret code. And what the hell did Santa know?

Obviously not enough. It was going to take more than a few Christmas carols and a stocking full of sheet ash to repair the damage that he'd done to her. There were no songs to sing, no words that he could say

And then Eric began to smile.

Yes, there were. They were buried in his closet, stuffed in a shoebox between an old tennis trophy and a pair of never-used hip waders.

He took the steps two at a time, tipping his head to St. Nick in the lobby. Maybe, maybe. He hadn't let himself dare to hope, to dream, until now. Maybe it was the Christmas tree, maybe it was the twinkle in Santa's eye. Maybe it was the piece of his heart that finally clicked firmly into place.

CHLOE TOLD HERSELF that she didn't care. It didn't matter that he had left. It was better this way. He didn't love her. He had never loved her. He didn't love her fat, he didn't love her beautiful. In the end, Eric Marshall and Chloe Skidmore would never be together forever.

The world didn't roll that way, no matter what fantasies she wove, and it was time that she wised up and moved away.

Time to leave Pine Crest for good.

But first, one small bit of business. She called the police department, and spoke to a very nice lieutenant. In detail, she explained that it was Teague Price who had torched the old mansion. Teague Price who had torched her home.

But not her home any longer.

After she hung up, she stared at the meager possessions that she'd brought with her to Pine Crest. Her great plan for revenge.

Ha!

She had an apartment in Baltimore. She knew that, and a tidy business making curtains and doing room design. Furious with herself, she threw open her suitcase and stuffed her perfect J. Mendel dress back into the tiniest pocket where she couldn't see it. She wasn't going to destroy it. It'd cost her too much money, and while Chloe felt comfortable destroying Marshall property, she was a little smarter with her own.

Her toothbrush joined her dress, and the black silk underwear that she'd bought only for him. Ha.

Like she'd ever let him see it again. Not in this lifetime and not in the next. As she scraped her toiletries off the sink, she muttered to herself, condemning the Marshall family to all sorts of vile punishments involving scorpions and ants and mosquitoes, mostly localized in the lower regions of the body, metaphorically speaking, of course.

Just as she finished, her belongings all gathered, and the last of her great revenge plot zipped shut, she heard a sound outside her door. At first she thought it was the carolers, but this was something different. Carolers didn't sound like Savage Garden. They didn't sing "Truly Madly Deeply" at Christmastime.

And then she caught the sound of a new voice. Louder, not so perfect, but the words were clear. Eric Marshall was singing outside her door, and judging by the loud yelling, the other hotel residents weren't very happy, but he didn't stop. He sang about loving her with every breath that he took, and Chloe felt herself tremble. She slid down against the door, to really listen to the words, to hope against hope that this wasn't a dream, that it wasn't a wish, that it wasn't just a fantasy. And just when she had convinced herself that maybe it was real, the music died. The people next door yelled, *"Thank God!"* Then a new song began.

The next one was the Backstreet Boys, "As Long As You Love Me." He showed some real boy-band potential on that one, although the hotel security guard didn't see it that way. Until he realized who was singing.

"Mr. Marshall? You feeling okay? We can take you downstairs, let you sleep it off."

"I'm not drunk."

"'Course not, sir."

"Chloe!"

She stayed silent for a long, long time, still not trusting this. Not trusting her ears, her mind, but in the end it was her heart that she put her faith in, and she cracked open the door.

"Yes?"

"I love you."

Then she slammed the door in his face.

He knocked on the door again, louder. "Chloe?"

She cracked open the door. "Yes?"

"I love you."

She slammed the door again.

They went through this four times before she finally realized that this time, he wasn't going to walk away.

This time when she cracked open the door, she invited him inside her room. To talk. They had a lot to talk about. Twelve years' worth of talk, and Chloe was determined that she wasn't going to be easy. Not this time. So she stayed in the wing chair near the window and waited for him to speak.

"Do you love your husband?"

"No," she confessed.

He grinned at that. "Good. Santa bets he was an ass. You can get a divorce. Oh, God, do you want to get a divorce?"

"I don't need to get a divorce."

He looked at her, clearly offended. "Yes, you do. You're mine. In the eyes of this town. In my eyes and the eyes of the law, you have to get a divorce. I don't do that. Except for that one time. Twice. Maybe three times, however you want to count it, but I have principles. I'm a Marshall."

Chloe took a deep breath, and blurted out the truth. "I don't have a husband. It was fake. I wanted to come back, to show you, to show everybody that I'd got the guy of my dreams."

She'd braced herself for anger, or some other "she's done it again" sort of reaction, but he only looked relieved.

"Thank God. I am so not an adulterer."

"What's your father going to say?"

Eric laughed. "Nothing good. We'll go to the gala. The Firemen's Ball is tonight, remember? You'll wear the family diamonds, and then I get to introduce you and watch his eyes pop out of their sockets."

"So you can get back at him? Is this another rebellion?"

"Another rebellion? I've never rebelled against my father in my life. Passive-aggressive, all the way. No, this is about me recovering the love of my life, and getting the added pleasure of having my parents admit that I am my own man."

"You always have been."

"In a very passive-aggressive sort of way."

He was smiling, and happy, and his heart was there in his eyes. "Do you love me because I'm skinny now? And beautiful?"

"Yes."

Her mouth fell open, and Eric laughed.

"Do you know when I made that tape for you, Chloe?"

"I'm hoping twelve years ago, because if you just now cranked it out, this relationship is over."

He came and sat on the floor by her feet, and took her hand, tracing over the place where the wedding ring had been. "Actually, it was thirteen. I'm a little slow that way."

It was odd seeing a Marshall at her feet, not the traditional way of things, and Chloe felt a fluttering in her heart. "I love that you're slow that way."

"You love me because I'm slow?" The hard gray eyes were lit within. Twin points of melted silver were burning. For her.

"Yes," she admitted happily.

"You love me?"

"I have always loved you. From the day I took my first breath. And I will love you until I take my last breath. There is no other man for me. There never will be."

He pulled at her hand, pulled her down to the carpet, where they were eye to eye. Heart to heart. "Stay with me, Chloe Skidmore. Stay here. Stay home. Forever."

He met her halfway, their lips touching, and outside the sweet strains of "We Wish You A Merry Christmas" rang in her ears. It was going to be a Merry Christmas. The very best Christmas ever.

* * * *

CANDACE
HAVENS

A HOT DECEMBER NIGHT

To my mom for all the wonderful Christmases,
and Heather Long for showing me
how blessed I am she is my friend.

1

ASSISTANT FIRE CHIEF Jason Turner commits mass murder during Christmas gala committee meeting!

Jason imagined what the other headlines would be if he had to endure one more minute of this meeting with the most argumentative people on Earth.

Argumentative and crazy.

The pillars of Pine Crest loved to listen to themselves talk. Their voices pinged off the brick walls of the conference room at the courthouse to the point where they sounded like a bunch of angry birds shrieking at one another.

Kill me now! he begged the universe.

You're an evil Grinch.

Yes, and I have every reason to be.

This time of year made him edgy. Whenever he turned a corner, or the phone rang or someone gave him a strange look, Jason worried that the Christmas curse would hit again. Nothing ever seemed to go right this time of year.

His grandfather had lost the family farm in a poker game on Christmas Eve forty years ago. His grandmother died on Christmas just two years ago. And being a fireman he'd seen the worst the holiday had to offer. Family homes destroyed by a string of lights, or stockings hung too close to the fire.

In his book, being forced to attend these meetings was a form of the curse. He adored these women when he had to deal with them one at a time. But all of them in the same room together was his version of hell.

Matchmakers. Busybodies. Mommies. Grandmothers with eligible and some not-so-eligible granddaughters, nieces and more. Women who liked to fix problems could be handled one at a time. Together, the pack could turn on him.

The throbbing in his head intensified.

They were hashing out details for the fundraiser to rebuild the Price Mansion, which had been significantly damaged in a recent fire. Jason had saved a life that night, but the fire still haunted him. They all did. He always wondered if there was more he and his team could have done.

Jason rubbed his temple.

Old Mrs. Randolph bumped his leg under the table for the third time. The bumps were followed by a pat on his knee. If she weren't close to ninety he might be worried she was flirting with him.

The chief must really hate me.

The Firemen's Annual Christmas Eve Ball committee had approached the chief first. He told them he was "too busy," and that Jason would be more than happy to take his place.

Too busy. Right.

Maybe too busy playing online poker and eating Christmas cookies the town widows had made him. Even with the peanut-butter gut, as the chief called the roll around his belly, the old man was still a catch—at least according to the widows. That wasn't saying much. There weren't many bachelors in Pine Crest.

"Assistant Chief Turner, what are your thoughts on the auction at the ball?" The sweet and sexy voice of Kristen Lovejoy broke through his reverie. The party planner was perfect in almost every way with her curly blond hair, voluptuous figure and sky-blue eyes that seemed to know way too much for a woman her age. Perfect, except for her passion for the holidays.

She was the one who always brought Christmas snacks and little holiday surprises for the committee. This was a committee meeting, not a party. And she was so cheerful. Jason had never seen her without a smile on her face.

Everyone stared at him. Jason cleared his throat and searched for something to say. "If you want men to bid, you're going to need stuff guys like," he said quickly, as though he'd been thinking about it all along.

"Stuff?" She gave him a sweet smile but her eyebrow rose as if she knew she had caught him daydreaming.

"Yes, autographed pictures of sports stars, or memorabilia. I have a friend who might be able to help us out with some of that, and I know the fire chief has a huge collection. He might be willing to donate something for such a good cause." That would teach the old man to shove him into these miserable committee meetings.

"And you might want to check with Lana over at the travel agency to see if she could offer a free cruise. I bet that would bring in a lot of cash." Jason was on a roll.

Glancing around the table he noticed the women had their mouths gaping open.

"What? Did I say something wrong?" Jason sat up straighter in his chair. Why were they looking at him like that?

Kristen cleared her throat. "Um, no. That was— That is to say, those are wonderful ideas. Would you like to talk to the chief about the donation?"

"Oh, no. That's not a good idea. Not to be sexist, but a pretty face would go a long way in getting him to give up some of his prized possessions."

"Very well," said Mrs. Peterson who had the look of a raven about her. The town librarian, she had a beaklike nose and eyes as black as coal. Jason wasn't afraid of much, but the older woman gave him pause. "Kristen, you'll talk to the chief. Mr. Turner, it's nice that you were able to contribute something."

Jason bit back a smile. He had to admit he had done little the last few meetings other than sit and stare at Kristen. She was a prize in their town and the men had to be lining up to take her out. What chance did he really have? He could throw his hat in the ring, but then would have to put up with the town gossips watching his every move.

"We'll get together again on Friday afternoon at 3:00 p.m.," the old raven said. "Meeting adjourned."

He let out a breath he didn't realize he'd been holding. Finally. He had just enough time to go home, change out of his uniform and get ready for poker night with the guys. Mike Reynolds would not be taking any part of Jason's paycheck this week. He had a strategy, which involved getting that lucky Mike drunk and sending him home in a taxi. No one ever said poker was fair, and Jason needed all the help he could get. His brother, Jeb, had called Jason the worst poker player ever; unfortunately, he wasn't wrong. But Jason loved the game.

"Mr. Turner?" That voice again. Where the other women sounded like vultures screeching, Kristen's voice was like a puffy white cloud that settled gently around him.

What was it about her? They had shared a few commiserating glances over the last week, and he'd been curious about her since the first day she'd been introduced to the committee. He admired the way she handled these women, and her patience was that of Job. Still, she always managed to push through on her agenda and get what she wanted.

He didn't know much about her except that she'd quit some corporate party planning job in Manhattan and moved to Pine Crest six months ago. Word was her mother had a house here, but it had been vacant for years. While Jason didn't believe in gossip, it was helpful when one wanted to know about beautiful women who'd arrived in town.

More than once he had thought about asking her out, but there was something about her that screamed commitment. She wasn't like the women he usually dated. And he wasn't looking for anything long-term.

Maybe that's why you can't stop thinking about her. She's off-limits.

He pushed in his chair. "Please, call me Jason." He wanted to hear her say his name.

She gave him a quick nod. "Jason, I wondered if I might ask you a few questions about the memorabilia. Are you available for coffee?"

The smoky gaze she gave him caught him off guard, but his body reacted accordingly.

Was she asking him out? Did he dare? It occurred to him that spending time with her wasn't the best idea for his sanity.

It's just coffee.

She smiled and he knew he would do whatever she wanted. He had a feeling he could deny this woman nothing, and it scared him.

"If you're busy, perhaps another time," she said quickly.

He opened the door for her. "No. I mean, I have time," Jason clarified. The boys could wait on him, and Jeb had a key. "I have something this evening, but I have a few minutes now. Let's go to the Java Express."

"That sounds good," she said.

The Java Express was busy, but Carrie, who dated one of the volunteer firemen at the station, was at the counter. She motioned them forward. There was a bit of grumbling until the customers saw it was Jason. Then the patrons waved and smiled.

"They must really like you," Kristen said after placing her order.

Jason motioned to a table. "Misguided hero worship. They don't seem to understand that it's my job to pull people out of burning buildings."

"Ahhh. That girl in the Price Mansion. Yes, that was quite heroic. I hear she's doing well."

"She's fine." This kind of thing made him uncomfortable. He didn't like people calling attention to his work. And to him, that's all it was. A job. He liked to help people. Some people worked at homeless shelters, he ran into burning buildings. He didn't understand why everyone made such a big deal out of it.

"So what is it you wanted to talk to me about?" Jason asked before sipping his coffee, which was black with one sugar.

Kristen sipped one of the popular Christmas drinks with peppermint and mocha. Jason had stopped himself from scowling at her when she ordered. He didn't know why people drank stuff that tasted like candy and had very little to do with coffee.

"The auction," she said. "Is there a certain approach I should take with the chief? And I needed to get the number of your friend so I can talk to him about a donation."

Jason chuckled. "Smile," he said.

"What?" Her eyebrows furrowed in confusion.

"When dealing with the chief. A smile will go a long way."

"Ah. I see." She grinned at him.

His lower extremities took notice. It would not do to have tented pants in the middle of Java Express. So Jason looked down at his coffee cup rather than her remarkably pretty face with the high cheekbones and kissable lips that called out to him.

"And your friend? The one with the collection?"

"Marcus," Jason said. The man might be one of his best friends but he didn't want him anywhere near Kristen.

That made him stop.

Why would he be jealous if Marcus was interested in Kristen?

The answer came quickly. Who knew what that smooth talker could convince her to do, and he felt protective of her. "I'll deal with him," he said.

She wrote down something on a notepad. "Can you let me know by Friday what he might have to offer? I thought, perhaps, we could put some of the items up on our website to help generate interest."

"Sure. Sure. I'll talk to him about it tonight," he promised.

Was that scent her? It was a mix of vanilla and cinnamon. Did she taste the same? Jason had a distinct urge to find out right in the middle of the coffee shop.

He swallowed hard. He had to get out of there before he made a fool of himself.

"Well, I need to get back to the station," he lied, but saying he had a poker game didn't seem right. Technically, he did have paperwork he needed to do and he was stopping by the station to pick up the chief, who insisted on going when he heard about the game.

She glanced up at him surprised. "Okay. Thanks for your help." She stuck out her hand. He held it in his for a few seconds before shaking it. Her skin was soft and creamy. His thumb brushed across her knuckles.

Her eyes flashed bigger, but she didn't yank away from him.

He continued to hold her hand for a little longer than necessary and realized he had no intention of letting her go.

Oh, crap.

"Is there something wrong?" she asked.

Jason shook his head. "No. That is… Um, would you like to go out on Friday night?"

Smooth.

Why had he done that? Why was his mouth saying the exact opposite of what his brain told him?

She smiled sweetly and he knew exactly why he'd done it.

SANTA COULD HAVE landed on her table in the middle of the Java Express and Kristen would not have been more surprised. Assistant Fire Chief Jason Turner had just asked her out.

Oh, heck yes.

No. No. Remember. You heard the rumors. He's a womanizer.

Even though no one had seen him date women in Pine Crest. Word was he liked to keep his private life private.

And he was definitely not her type. She usually went for slightly nerdy guys, who seemed as though they would be safe, stable partners.

How has that worked out for you so far?

She'd been engaged to safe, and he'd turned out to be a real jerk.

Why shouldn't she go out with Jason? Didn't she deserve a little fun? She'd promised herself the next relationship would be about fun. No commitment. No strings. Just fun.

And Jason was definitely the man for that.

"That would be lovely. We can talk about the charity aspect of the ball. Where did you have in mind?" She couldn't believe how calm she sounded. This man had been the star of many a late-night fantasy for her, and now he had asked her out. But she had mentioned the gala in case it wasn't really a date. Maybe he only wanted to talk to her more about the auction items and she had jumped to conclusions.

"We'll go some place nice for dinner." He finally let go of her hand, and it was as though she had been set adrift. When he'd touched her, her body had tingled from head to toe.

"I'll pick you up at your house. Say seven-thirty?"

"Sure." She put her number in his cell phone and handed

it to him. Then she watched him leave. In his uniform or out of it, the assistant chief could stop traffic. In addition to being male model material with his square jaw and chocolate-brown hair, he had a body that had stopped her cold ever since she had been hired to plan the ball.

And he had asked her out.

What am I going to talk to him about? What will I wear?

It was one thing to be surrounded by committee members discussing a charity event. It was quite another to be alone with a man like Jason Turner. Callie, her best friend, called him pure sex.

Her mind had a field day trying to figure it out exactly what Callie had meant by pure sex. She'd had okay sex, and not-so-great sex. But she'd never had pure sex.

Though sex in general was all she could think of when he was around. At the meetings she had to take notes so that she was forced to concentrate on what was being said. Otherwise she would have leaped over the table and devoured him long ago.

As if. She checked herself. Kristen was not exactly known as the most assertive woman in the world. She was no doormat, but she wasn't overly courageous when it came to men. Two bad relationships with selfish men would do that to a girl.

But Jason was different. She had watched how he handled those women in the meetings. Kind, he had a way about him that sent those women aflutter every time he spoke. He might be a womanizer, but he was one who knew how to treat a lady.

And he asked you out.

She still couldn't believe it.

Her stomach roiled with nerves. She only had three days to get ready. It wasn't long enough. Sure, she could throw a huge charity ball with only two weeks' preparation including food, auction and music. But this date was the biggest thing she had to tackle in a long time. There was no time to shop for a new dress. Panic rose in waves.

She pulled her cell from her purse and dialed the only person who might help.

"I have a date!"

JASON STACKED the files neatly on his desk. There would be time to deal with them in the morning before the staff meeting. He had a poker game to host.

"Jason?" The chief stood at his door.

He stood. "Sir." What could the old man want now? It was just like him to wait until the last minute to pile more work on Jason knowing they had a poker game to get to.

"I hear you're going on a date with the party planner for the gala."

How in the heck had he found that out? Jason didn't think Kristen was the kind of woman who would run around telling people about their date.

"Is that a problem?"

"Only if you don't treat her right. Kristen's the daughter of a good friend of mine, and she's a good girl. Before he passed away, I promised I'd look out for her. She's not one of those women you *normally* date."

The older man had a point. The last woman Jason dated tried to pin him with a paternity suit, even though they had protected sex. The kid wasn't his, which was proven with a DNA test. But it didn't matter. The chief, of course, had blamed Jason for the choices he made. Jason couldn't argue with that. His choices had been his choices. And after that whole episode, Jason had had to do some real soul-searching.

Wait. The chief knew Kristen? Why had she asked for his help in approaching him? That was something he'd have to ask on their date.

"She is a good person, which is why I asked her out," Jason

said. The bite in his tone had the chief lifting an eyebrow. "You should be happy, I'm taking your advice. I'm dating someone you'd approve of for a change."

"No funny stuff. You hear me? I've known this girl since she was a baby." The chief gave Jason the evil eye, and Jason had to turn away so the old man wouldn't see him smile.

"Yes, sir." Jason coughed to hide a laugh.

And he told the truth. He had no plans for funny stuff. No, what he wanted to do to Kristen was serious business. He couldn't wait to see what her lips tasted like when he kissed her, or how she'd react when his hand slipped up—

"I'll be keeping an eye on you, boy."

Splash. Just like that, ice-cold water on his very warm thoughts.

"And the next time you want to ask a young woman out, don't do it in the middle of a coffee shop. The whole town is buzzing. I'll grab my gear and we can go. I'm ready to win all your money."

Jason sighed.

He loved small-town living, but times like this made him wonder why he had ever stayed on after his dad recovered.

Now, he had to date the woman of his dreams—at least, his dreams from the last few weeks—with the whole town watching.

Well, since I'm going to do this, I should give them something to talk about.

Jason smiled at the chief's back.

2

Kristen stared at the mirror in horror. "No, no, no." Tears streamed down her face and onto the towel wrapped around her shoulders.

She sniffled. "Universe. Why do you hate me? Why? I'm a good person. I'm kind to old people and animals. I go to church, well, sometimes. I help those in need." The last few words came out in a blubbery cry.

She sat down on the edge of her bathtub and let the tears fall. There had been no time to go to the salon, so she'd bought a box of color to brighten her locks a bit. Oh, it was bright. Gone was the dishwater blond, in its place was off-white cotton the texture of straw. Her silky hair, one of her only decent features, was a complete and total mess.

I have to cancel the date.

There was no other choice. She could not go out with the hottest guy in town with hair that looked like it belonged on the floor of a manger.

She searched for her cell phone. Then it hit her. She had given Jason her number, but she had no way of getting in touch with him. And he would be by any minute.

Flinging herself into action, she grabbed the blow-dryer. Once the mess was dry, she twisted it into a tight chignon.

Then she sprayed on half a bottle of hairspray to make the cottony bits stay down.

Hopefully, I won't be near any open flames.

The result was something that looked like a flattened cotton ball, but it would have to do. She painted smoky gray on her eyelids, and lined them with kohl. Maybe he would notice her face, rather than her insane hair.

Of course, she still had the killer dress.

The halter neckline and pencil skirt made her figure look decent, for once. She had worried that she would look like she was trying too hard, but her friend Callie had demanded she wear it. Telling her that she should go out with guns blazing.

Shimmying into the dress she stopped. "You've got to be kidding." Those darn Christmas cookies she couldn't resist eating made it difficult to slip the dress over her hips. "Great." She ran for the dresser and pulled on the tightest Spanx she could find. The dress finally fit over her hips.

"Who needs to breathe?" she muttered as she slipped on her favorite bracelet. The silver bracelet was adorned with six tiny silver presents with delicate ribbons of velvet.

The front doorbell rang and Bibi barked. "Calm down, girl. He's one of the good guys." She stepped into the black heels she'd purchased, only teetering slightly as she made her way to the door.

Jason was dressed in a black suit and white shirt. She had never seen him in anything but his uniform or jeans. But this suit—well, she needn't worry about anyone noticing her passed out on the floor with her cotton head in flames, because all eyes would be on him.

"Hey," she said as casually as possible. "Do you want to come in?"

Bibi howled from the kitchen.

He laughed. "Are you sure it's safe? It sounds like the hell-hounds aren't too excited about me being here."

"Oh, Bibi is as loud as they come, but she's a sweet girl. She just likes people to know she's around so she can lick them to death. Besides, she's blocked in the kitchen with the gate. Let me grab my coat and we can go."

She fumbled with the hall closet doorknob. She picked her black pea coat off the hanger. It didn't exactly go with her outfit, but it was twenty degrees outside and she needed warmth.

"It's a shame to cover up such a beautiful dress," Jason said as he helped her on with her jacket.

"Oh, thank you." She flicked a hand as if she wore this kind of thing every day. "I'm glad you showed up in a suit. I was worried I might be overdressed."

She sucked in a breath when his hand touched her neck as he helped straighten the collar of her coat.

Jeez. Get a grip.

"You go all out for the holidays. Those are a lot of lights outside, and from here I can see three Christmas trees." He didn't sound happy about it.

She shrugged. "I love this time of year. The twinkle lights and lawn reindeer. Every once in a while you see people being kind to one another. It makes me feel better about life. Don't you love it?"

There was a long pause. "I—don't really *do* holidays." Jason waited for her to lock the door.

Maybe she heard him wrong. "You don't *do* holidays? Is it a religious thing?" She slapped a hand over her mouth. "I mean—I didn't mean to insult you."

Jason shrugged. "You didn't. My family doesn't have much luck with holidays, even though my mom refuses to give up. She and Dad live just outside of town and turn the farm into Santa's workshop. The kids around here love it, but after growing up with all that, I'm burned out. And then there's the commercialism.

"I don't understand why people have to wait until the holidays to be nice to one another. And because people aren't careful about using lights and candles, we see a surge in house fires. It's devastating for the families involved."

Kristen had never thought of it that way. "I can see why you feel the way you do. But—" She forgot what she was about to say. A new dilemma had presented itself.

He opened the door of the truck and she stood there for a moment. In order to get in his truck, she needed to hike a leg up on the sideboard. But the dress would not allow it.

Great. Now what do I do?

He stood there patiently waiting for her.

"I—uh. I can't get in," she said honestly.

"Did you forget something?" He touched her shoulder.

"No, I mean my dress is so tight I can't physically climb in."

She glanced up, and there wasn't even a hint of a smile on his face.

His brow furrowed and his lips were a straight line. "I'm sorry. I didn't even think of it. I should have borrowed Jeb's sedan. If you don't mind, I may have a solution."

At this point she wanted nothing more than to run back in her house and crawl under the covers. Well, right after she tore off the Spanx, which were causing her to breathe funny. Or maybe that was Jason.

"Okay," she said, mortified.

"Turn around and put your hands on my shoulders."

So far this wasn't such a bad plan after all. She touched his shoulders and heat surged through her.

"Pardon me," he said as he slid his big hands around her waist and lifted her gently into the truck.

"Thank you." She scooted her legs around to the front. "And please don't apologize. If my dress wasn't so—"

"Perfect," he said. "And if I forgot to say it, you look beautiful."

Heat spread across her cheeks, and she was grateful for the

dark interior. The men she usually dated didn't say things like that. She didn't know how to respond.

He climbed in the other side. "I wanted to ask you something."

"Sure," she said grateful for the change in subject.

"Why did you ask about how to approach the chief? He says he's known you since you were a kid."

She laughed.

"I guess it's time to come clean. He was a friend of my dad. I wanted to talk to you apart from the committee. And that's what came out of my mouth at the time. I'm not normally the kind of girl who asks a man out for coffee and I was nervous."

"Yeah, I was kind of surprised, but I'm glad. To be honest, I had the same problem when I asked you out to dinner," he said. "I wondered if you might be too busy with the gala to go out with me."

As if. She stopped herself from snorting.

"So, did you grow up here?" he asked. Surely he'd have seen her before now. "I don't remember seeing you before."

"We lived here when I was a baby. My dad grew up in Pine Crest and thought it would be a great place to raise a kid. When he was killed in the first Gulf War, mom rented out the house and we moved in with my grandmother in Soho, in New York City, so she could pursue her creative and religious interests. I was five." She rolled her eyes.

"Rough childhood?" He turned onto the main road in town.

She thought for a moment. "No. If I'm honest, she provided a well-rounded education for me. We traveled the world in the summers and I attended one of the best private schools in Manhattan during the school year thanks to my grandmother. Mom just wasn't the most stable person. I spent a lot of time with my grandmother and my nanny. In fact, when I considered college, I stuck close to home in case my mom needed me. Luckily, my grandmother the party planner used to let me work with her part time and that sort of stuck. I guess it was a different way than most kids grow up, but it wasn't bad.

"It must have been great growing up in a small town like this where you know everyone and they know you." She changed the focus to him.

Jason chuckled. "I'd say it had its good points, but sometimes, especially when you're a kid, you'd like to get away with something without someone calling your mother to tell her what you did."

This time she laughed.

"I left as soon as I could and went to school in Buffalo. My dad had always been a volunteer fireman, and I decided that's what I wanted to do. I worked all over the Northeast, and then dad got sick and they needed help with the farm. So I took a job here."

"Oh, no. Is he okay?"

"The old coot had a miraculous recovery once I came home. Truth be told, he had been really sick. But when my brother and I moved back home his heart seemed to grow a lot stronger. Nothing like parental guilt to keep you close by.

"Ah, here we are."

He picked Matilda's in the center of town. While the name might indicate home cooking, Chef Max, who named the restaurant after his mother, served a different gourmet menu every night. It was the kind of place most people went to celebrate anniversaries and other special occasions.

Secretly pleased that he'd picked one of the nicest places in town, Kristen was grateful to him for setting her back down on the ground when they arrived. The hostess who showed them to their table only noticed Jason, and Kristen decided that was as it should be. The town hero looked good enough to eat.

The more she looked at him, the more she thought they should skip the meal and go straight for dessert.

He'd been so sweet when he talked about his family. She knew they probably gave each other a hard time, but they all loved one another. She and her mother were polite to each other, but they didn't have much of a relationship.

She and Jason were escorted to a quiet corner table, one of the best in the place. The hostess lingered a bit too long but Jason kindly sent her on her way to find their waiter.

"I'm sorry about that," Jason said. "She's the sister of a friend, and she's been following us around since we were kids. We spent many a summer day trying to figure out ways we wouldn't have to take her with us."

"She's, um, very animated." Kristen did not believe in gossiping or saying bad things about people. From an early age she had believed in Karma, thanks to one of her mother's many religious explorations. The idea of Karma was one that stuck, and it was something she worried about constantly.

"I guess that's one way to put it. I hope you don't mind the restaurant. I was in the mood for steak, and they have some of the best." He paused as if he realized something. "I—uh—also wanted to take you somewhere nice. You know, that first date stuff you do to impress a woman."

Like he needed help doing that.

She grinned. "First date stuff?"

"You take the girl out to a nice place and pretend like you know what you're doing. When the truth is, you have no idea what to say or do. And you just fake it and hope she doesn't notice."

"Jason, are you nervous?"

He shrugged.

Her smile grew. She couldn't believe it. Could he really be this down-to-earth? Maybe it was all a part of his game.

She didn't care. She was ready to play.

"Well, it's nice to know I'm not the only one. Between the

fiasco with my dress, and, well, let's talk about the elephant in the room. My hair is a scary mess."

"First of all, there's not a thing wrong with that dress. You look incredible. And I thought your hair was one of those holiday things girls do."

Was it possible for a man to be so kind? Most of the guys she dated in the past would have made a joke about how she looked.

A blush crept along her cheeks again. He had a habit of doing that to her. "Thank you for that. So what kind of steak do you like?" She opened the menu desperate to get the focus off herself.

What is wrong with me? Usually, she chose her words carefully and she was never this honest about herself. Her mother's flightiness and need to say whatever was on her mind had the opposite effect on Kristen. Like anyone else, she had bad days, but she didn't see that as a reason to make everyone else around her miserable by sharing her troubles.

People accused her of being eternally cheerful, but she didn't see that as a bad thing.

"I'm fond of beef in general, but particularly fond of the Porterhouse here," he answered.

Kristen had a great affinity for all types of food. Steak with a baked potato was one of her favorite meals. There was just one problem.

"If you don't like beef," Jason eyed her hesitantly, as if this was some kind of test. "They have fish or—"

"No, I love steak." So what if she busted out of her dress in the middle of the nicest restaurant in town? That would certainly give the women on the committee something to talk about. She had never seen women who gossiped so much. She was under constant scrutiny.

For years the local women had planned the gala on their own. It had been the mayor's wife's idea to bring in a professional planner to take the party to the next level with the fundraising component. They were trying to rebuild the Price Mansion, which had a great deal of historical significance for the town.

But Kristen, being new blood, had found making changes a constant struggle. She saw so many ways to make their event more successful, but she had to be clever about how she proposed those ideas.

Jason stared at her as if he were waiting for her to answer. "Steak. Yes. I'm more of a rib-eye or a filet mignon kind of girl."

The wary expression on Jason's face changed. He nodded at their waiter who had just arrived. "Bill, good to see you. How is Beth doing?"

The other man laughed. "She is as big as a house, and happy as can be."

Kristen's eyebrows furrowed. She didn't know who Beth was, but she had a feeling she wouldn't appreciate being called as big as a house.

"Bill's wife is about to deliver twins, any day now. We've done two practice runs with the EMTs," Jason said as an explanation. "If they're on another call, we go as backup."

The waiter patted Jason's shoulder. "Your patience with the two of us hasn't gone unappreciated."

"Hey, with twins you never know," Jason said seriously. "It's better to know how long it takes for us to respond in case you aren't there to get her to the hospital in time. Or if she goes into labor too fast, which can happen with twins."

"Well, it's great that you guys are so nice about it," Bill said.

Jason waved a hand. "Hey man, if it eases Beth's mind it is worth it."

Bill cleared his throat.

"Well, let me recommend a good wine and tell you about

some of the specials, so you two can get on with your date." Bill explained what they had available, but she only caught half of what he said.

From the conversation, she gathered that the wife had called the fire station. They must receive calls like that all the time and Jason had been so patient. It scared her how perfect he was. He didn't seem to have an ego. Everyone in town called him a hero, and he was. But he didn't act like it.

She kept waiting for Mr. Hyde to pop out of him. The man had to have some flaws.

"Do you want wine with your steak? And did you want the rib-eye or filet?" Jason asked.

"The filet would be great, and maybe a burgundy," she said to Bill. But she moved her hand and nearly knocked over one of the water glasses. She caught it before it spilled. Distracted, she didn't notice what happened with her other hand.

Before she knew it, Jason was holding a wet napkin around her wrist.

Ripping the bracelet off her wrist, he dumped it in his water.

"You caught your ribbons on fire." A small poof of steam came from the glass.

Really? Could this night get any better?

She glanced up to find Bill doing his best to stifle a laugh. He cleared his throat. "I'll get those steaks going and bring out your wine."

"The skin is reddened. I have a kit in my truck."

"No," she said quickly.

How many times did she have to be mortified before she took the hint? She had no business being on a date with this man. This was the universe telling her she was out of her depth.

"It's fine." She stood and there was a distinct ripping sound down the back of her dress. Now, the only thing between her rear and the patrons of the restaurant was the nude-colored Spanx she'd pulled on at the last minute. "Yes. Um. Excuse me."

She took the wet napkin and placed it behind her, hoping it covered at least part of her backside.

This is not happening to me. I'm going to wake up and this is going to be the terrible nightmare you have the night before a big event.

Only she wasn't asleep.

I can't do this.

She pulled out her cell phone. "Time to call in the cavalry."

The first ten minutes, Jason assumed she was trying to fix her dress. He worked on restoring the bracelet, but there wasn't much he could do. Two of the presents were toast. He was worried she might not be taking proper care of the small burns on her wrist. He'd moved as quickly as possible with the water to minimize the damage to her, but red marks on her arm had been proof he hadn't been fast enough.

Some fireman you are.

After fifteen minutes he sent one of the waitresses to the ladies room to make sure she was doing okay.

"Sir, she isn't in there," the waitress said when she returned.

Jason sat back in his chair and frowned. She'd run out on him. He was sure that had never happened to him before. Though he should be angry, he couldn't imagine what she must be going through. She'd burned her bracelet and ripped her dress. She had been upset over getting in the truck.

It had probably been the worst date she'd ever been on. He couldn't blame her for dumping him.

But he wasn't about to give up.

"Can you tell Bill to get the check for me, and box the meals?" he asked the waitress.

He waited an hour before he returned to her house. All of the lights were on so he knew she was home.

As he reached her porch, a howl came from within.

Jason ran for the door, but it was locked. He pounded on it. "Kristen!"

He jostled the handle again.

Lifting his foot he was about to kick in the door when it swung open wide.

The vision before him was not at all what he'd expected.

Kristen stood before him wrapped in nothing but a pink silk robe, a short one that showed off her amazingly long legs.

"What are you doing here?" She didn't look happy to see him.

"I—thought you might want dinner?" He lifted the bags in his hand.

"You brought me food even though I ran out on you?"

There was another howl.

He moved past her into the house without asking permission. "Do you have some kind of torture chamber in here or something?"

She stared at him as if he had three heads. "Oh, oh. No, it's Bibi. There's something wrong with her. I think she's sick. But the vet isn't open. I was about to change clothes and take her to an all-night animal clinic."

He sat the food on her dining room table. He tried not to notice the huge china cabinet with what seemed the largest collection of Santa Claus figurines he'd ever seen.

Bibi turned out to be a large black Chow, who was on the kitchen floor on a dog bed, panting. Her belly was distended, as if she'd eaten a watermelon. Her sad brown eyes had him kneeling down to present the back of his hand. He'd seen this sort of thing more than once growing up on his family's farm.

"If you have an old shower curtain, some old towels and a sheet, get them," he said.

"What's wrong with her?" Kristen asked worriedly. She hopped from foot to foot and he noticed she wore dark red nail polish on her toes. The color was quite different than the soft pink she wore on her fingernails. What other secrets did she have that he could uncover?

Mind out of the gutter, man.

"She's in labor."

"I— Uh. What?" Kristen's hand flew to her mouth. "I had her on a diet because I thought she was fat. I found her in the woods when I was trying to find a proper Christmas tree for the fundraiser. I called the pound, but they were overwhelmed, so I thought I would take care of her until I could find her a home. How could I have not known she was pregnant? I don't know how to deliver puppies."

"Well, I'm no expert, but most of the time Mother Nature takes its course in these situations. The best thing we can do is make sure she's comfortable. This could take several hours."

The dog eyed him with a wary glance, but he held his hand out for her to sniff again. She licked it. More than likely it had something to do with the fact that he'd been carrying steaks, but he'd take what he could get.

"I'll let you two get acquainted while I get the sheet and towels. Do we need anything else?" Kristen asked.

"Music. Something soothing. Animals respond well to music." He'd said soothing because he had a feeling, glancing around her house, that Christmas songs would be an automatic choice. He could take a lot, but not a never-ending litany of holiday tunes.

The music might go a long way in helping Bibi's owner to relax as well. He liked the fact that she hadn't flinched when he mentioned the dog was about to give birth on the new wooden floors of Kristen's kitchen. That was one of the reasons he asked for the shower curtain and sheet.

When she returned, her pink robe was gone and in its place

was a pair of flannel pajama bottoms with Santas on them, and a tank top with a hoodie. He wouldn't have thought anything could be sexier than the robe, but he was wrong. She'd washed off her makeup and she looked so young and fresh.

He cleared his throat, trying to get his mind back on the task at hand. "Right. We don't want to move her. That's a good way to get bitten, but we do need to get the shower curtain and then one of the towels underneath her hindquarters. She might like it better if you handled that. I'll do my best to distract her."

He petted the dog's head and Kristen gently centered the towels.

The dog made a strange "oomph" noise and her eyes closed.

"Ah, looks like we may be closer than I thought," Jason said.

"What do we do?"

"Nothing," Jason answered. "We wait and watch. If there's excessive bleeding or if she begins convulsing—"

"Convulsing!" Kristen cried. "We have to get her to the vet."

Jason grabbed her hand and pulled her down beside him. The smell of cinnamon and vanilla wafted around him.

The woman smelled good enough to— What had he been saying?

Oh, yeah, he was supposed to be comforting her about the dog.

"She'll be fine. She's lucky you found her or she'd be doing this out in the cold and those pups would have had little chance of survival."

Kristen shuddered, and he hugged her shoulders. "We will keep an eye on her. I promise, I won't let anything happen to her."

She relaxed against him. "I don't know what I would do

if you weren't here. In fact, why are you here? I walked out on you."

He chuckled. "This night didn't exactly go as expected for either of us. I decided to give you the benefit of the doubt."

"I can honestly say this was one of the worst dates ever." She laughed. "Wait, not because of you. But that dress and my hair. Well, I felt like the universe was conspiring against me."

"You might very well think that, considering what happened," he said. "But then, we wouldn't have been here to take care of Bibi during her time of need. Though I have a feeling she could have handled it all on her own."

"Do you have to be smart, too?" She sighed. "You're just too perfect."

Jason stifled a big laugh because he didn't want to bother Bibi. "You've got to be kidding. Look, I'm far from perfect. Believe me."

"That's not true." She glanced up and he saw that she was serious. "Those old women on the committee are putty in your hands. You showed up with a meal after I left you at the restaurant. And you're helping me with my pregnant dog. The only thing remotely strange about you is that you hate the holidays."

"There is that. And I spend most of those meetings wondering if I can get away with mass murder," he said honestly. "And I wasn't happy when you left, but I understood. I probably would have done the same under the circumstances. My guess is that your dress couldn't be repaired with a few safety pins, and you decided to sneak out the back."

She nodded against his shoulder.

"Mass murder?" she asked.

"Don't put me on a pedestal, Kristen. I told you, I'm far from perfect. Those women love to talk and I'm not one for sitting around much. I like doing things. If it hadn't been for you these last few weeks, I don't know what I would have done. You are the only bright spot in those dull meetings."

The way her face lit up when she smiled gave her an angelic quality. Jason was about to lean down and kiss her when there was a low "grrrrr."

"Ah, well, would you look at that," Jason motioned toward the dog. Bibi was licking the first pup.

"It's so tiny," Kristen squeaked. "I can't believe she had a baby and we didn't even see it happen. You're such a brave girl." Kristen made kissing noises at the dog.

"I didn't think the puppies would be so small. She's such a big dog." A tear slid down Kristen's cheek.

Jason thumbed it away. "Trust me, they grow fast. In six weeks, you'll be amazed how big they are."

In all, Bibi presented five pups. The dog was worn out by the ordeal, but the babies were already searching for milk and the dog's instincts kicked in as she nudged them toward her belly.

"I feel like an excited grandma." Kristen gasped. "They're all so beautiful."

They were squirming black-and-white balls of fur. "You may be a lot of things, but you are no grandma." Jason waggled his eyebrows teasing her.

She playfully punched him. "You know what I mean. I can't believe this. Now what do I do?"

"I don't know about you, but I'm really hungry. Let's wash up and eat, and I'll explain dog parenting 101 to you."

"Deal," she said taking his hand and pulling him up with her.

They were chest to chest.

Jason reached out and tucked an errant curl behind her ear. "You are more gorgeous every time I look at you."

She scoffed, "Now I know you're messing with me." She

pushed away, and grabbed the bags from the table. "I'll heat up the steaks."

But Jason hadn't been joking. She was a siren calling for his soul. He could feel it every time she looked at him.

And he was helpless to do anything about it.

3

SOMETHING WAS wrong. Kristen couldn't get her eyes to open, but the bed beneath her was hard and she'd lost the feeling in her right hand because it was under something. Without opening her eyes, she shook her hand and then settled it on the bed again.

"Sssst." A man sucked a breath through his teeth. Her eyes popped open. She was half on Jason and half on the couch. Her hand had landed in a somewhat precarious place and she lifted it quickly. Though not so fast that she didn't notice her favorite fireman had every right to be proud.

"Oh, sorry," Kristen apologized. Embarrassed, she shifted so she could leverage herself off the couch, but there was no way to do it without crawling across his body.

After hours of talking and watching a movie, they'd fallen asleep.

She had no idea how they'd ended up entangled like this.

"I don't mind." His rich male voice sent delicious tingles through her body. His lips found her ear and he feathered tiny kisses down her neck. Shivers of delight ran through her body.

Never in her life had she wanted something more than this man. She was tired of being a good girl, of never taking risks.

His mouth found hers and she was lost.

She sighed against him.

Yes, she was ready to be very, very bad.

Her hand once again slipped down to his manhood and she caressed him. Power surged through her as he moaned against her lips.

Jason slid his hand down to her waist. She fit so perfectly against him. It was almost as if he had been made exactly for her.

He shifted her so that she was on top of him, and she nearly lost it when his erection pressed against her heat.

Their tongues tested each other in a battle of wills, as if neither could get enough of the other.

His thumb teased her nipples to hard peaks. The friction between their bodies increased.

"Are you sure?" he asked as he removed her tank top and then her bra.

"Yes." Kristen traced a finger across his cheek.

His hands covered her breasts.

"Assistant Chief!" His radio squawked.

Kristen jumped as if someone was in the room with them. "You should respond," she said as she squirmed on top of him.

"It's W.T. No need to worry." His fingers continued to work their magic.

"Sir, I know you said no interruptions but—there's a fire. Thirty-nine Pebble Street," W.T. said nervously.

"Hell," Jason grumbled.

Kristen jumped up, and tossed the radio to him.

He gave her a quick glance as if to say he was sorry.

She smiled. "Go, go," she yelled.

Before she could say another word, Jason was out the door.

Racing to check on Bibi, she made certain the dog had food and water. Then she grabbed warmer clothes and a couple of blankets. She could maybe help him.

Her hands shook as she reached for her keys, but this was no time to cave.

Jason might need her.

And she had to make sure he was safe.

FROM KRISTEN'S FRONT door to the fire took Jason less than two minutes. But time was critical in these situations. There was a little girl standing in the yard wearing fuzzy pajamas with feet. She couldn't have been more than four or five.

"Who's in the house?" Jason knelt down beside her.

When she didn't answer right away, he touched her shoulder. This was a waste of time. Gray smoke permeated the air.

"I'm going to make sure your family is okay." Seconds counted so he headed for the door.

"Mommy and Brubbie," the little girl cried out. "I stopped and I rolled. I did. Promise."

The neighbors gathered around. "Get her a blanket and move to the other side of the street," he called over to them as he rushed into the house. If the house had natural gas, there could be an explosion any minute.

Jason ran to the kitchen on the left of the entry and wet the scarf he'd brought with him. He wound the wet scarf around his face. Normally, he would have extra gear in his truck, but he had loaned it to a new rookie, Jessie, until the other man's came in.

The house was fairly small, featuring an old Craftsman style. The fire was up high. Something had ignited in the attic and the old beams were going up fast.

He heard a scream and ran up the stairs two at a time. It was against the code to run in unprotected but there wasn't time to wait for his team.

Down a long hallway filled with smoke, he heard another muffled sound.

They were closer to the roof on this second story and he

could see the outside walls beginning to burn. The suffocating heat pressed in on him.

"Help," a voice so weak it was barely discernable came from out of the smoke.

Jason raced to the end of the hall and nearly tripped on the woman there.

"My leg. I can't walk. The baby." She coughed, and then passed out.

He didn't hear any baby, which was a very bad sign. He headed for the closest bedroom, crawling across the floor where the air was a bit clearer. He bumped into a piece of furniture. Raising his hand he felt spindles and realized it was a crib. He popped up on his knees and came face to face with a big pair of blue eyes.

"Hello, Brubbie," he said as he scooped up the baby and wrapped him in the blanket from the bedding on the crib. It looked new, which meant it was most likely treated with fire retardant.

The ceiling crashed down into the center of the room. Jason leaped to the doorway where the mother lay. He shook her lightly, but she didn't respond. Keeping the baby tight to his chest, he lifted the mother over his right shoulder. He struggled to stand, making sure he had his balance before he took a step. Smoke completely filled the hall. The scarf had fallen off of his nose and mouth, and breathing was difficult. Hands full, there was nothing he could do about it.

He took each step gingerly, making sure that the floorboards beneath him held. It was slow going and the heat had intensified. Those blue eyes were still open and interested in everything going on, and for that, Jason was grateful. He only hoped the mother fared as well. He couldn't tell if she was still breathing and he couldn't take the time to check if he were to save them.

It was a terrible dilemma, but they were all better off if

he could get them out of the house. There was another loud crash, and the flames roared behind him. Something hot hit his lower back and Jason took off. As he reached the top of the stairs, the attic fell into the second floor.

Jason navigated the last few steps, holding tight to the woman and the child. His muscles ached and burned as the house caved in around them. A huge deluge of freezing cold water drenched his face and head, cooling the pain on his back. The trucks had arrived.

"I'm here." There in the middle of the living room was Jessie, geared up and ready to go. He reached for the baby, but Jason shook his head.

"Out," ordered Jason. "Run!"

4

HEAT SEARED Jason's backside as he ran for the door. The rookie didn't have to be told twice. He was out the door with Jason on his heels as the house collapsed behind them. The other firemen raced up the steps. "Get back," he said hoarsely. "Roof's going down." He handed off the woman to one of the firefighters. The relief to his shoulder was instant.

Immediately, he ran the baby to the ambulance. His legs shook, but he continued on. At the ambulance he found the little girl from earlier sitting in Kristen's lap eating a Christmas cookie.

"Dat's him." She pointed to Jason. "He has Brubbie. I say I stopped and dropped. I did."

Kristen smiled. "You were so brave and good. And Brubbie is safe and sound."

The girl held out her arms for her brother.

Jason handed the baby to the EMTs. "They need to check to make sure your brother is breathing okay, and to make sure he's healthy," he told the child. Then he touched her head. "You were very brave. Your mother is going to be so proud of you."

He prayed the woman was still alive. His throat burned as if acid had been poured down it.

"Babies, where are my babies?" he heard the mother screech from the other ambulance. He thanked the stars she was alive. No child should have to live without his mother.

Though there where times when he wished someone would adopt him so he could get away from his.

Humor. It was the only way he got through most days.

Kristen looked so sweet sitting there with the child in her arms. He leaned down to kiss her cheek.

She frowned, and pushed his shoulder to turn him around. When he did she gasped.

"He's burned." Her voice trembled. When no one seemed to be listening, she said it a little louder. "Jason's back is burned. Help. Please."

"Oh, no," the child said. "You haz bad boo-boos. You needs the medicine."

One of the EMTs turned away from the baby and saw Jason. "Assistant Chief, have a seat," the woman ordered.

"I'm fine, Lisa. Take care of the child."

"That baby hasn't got a mark on him and his breathing sounds as strong as it comes. You, on the other hand, have had your shirt burned off your back and have at least some first-degree burns that I can see. So when I say sit, I mean sit."

"You've been bossy since kindergarten. Just because you're the chief's daughter— Ouch! What the heck are you doing? You did that on purpose," Jason grumbled.

"Shut it, lizard. Or I'll tell your new girlfriend here what you did in the eighth grade that got you three months of detention." She put an oxygen mask over his mouth.

"You children quit squabbling or I'll tell the chief," said Jason's friend Mike, the other EMT.

Jason pulled off the mask to complain.

"I can't believe you are going to marry this evil— Ouch! Lisa, stop it."

"Now, honey, be gentle with him. You know how sensitive he is," Mike teased.

The couple laughed out loud.

"You have to tell me that story," Kristen begged.

"Oh, you need to make him tell it," Lisa said. "If nothing else, to see what mortification looks like on a grown man."

Mike picked up the baby, who was reaching out for Jason.

"Looks like you made a friend," Lisa said. "The kid has no taste."

"Oh, no, little guy, you are going to go visit your mom. I think she'll heal a lot faster. In fact, let's take your big sis and do a family reunion," Mike suggested. "That is, if I can trust you not to rip off his skin in spite?" Mike gave his fiancée a serious look, and then ruined it by winking.

"Fine. I won't hurt him—much."

"Okay, little miss. Why don't we go see your mom?" Mike held out his hand. But the girl turned and held tight to Kristen's neck.

"I'll come with you," Kristen offered. "I want to meet your mom. You told me she makes better cookies than me, and I just don't know if I believe that," she teased.

Kristen followed Mike to the other ambulance.

Jason heard the woman crying with relief as she saw her children.

"For a big sissy, you were pretty darn brave in there," Lisa said. "Stupid. You could have gotten yourself killed going in unprotected like that. But brave just the same.

"And that girlfriend of yours must have it bad for you. The only thing that kept her from going in there after you was that little girl. Clingy kid would not let go of her. That's a good thing, otherwise your little hero worshipper, Jessie, was going to have to tackle her."

That was something he'd pay money to see.

She must have it bad for you.

Unfortunately, that feeling went both ways. This fun little thing he thought they were having had turned into something more in a very short time.

Jason wasn't sure how he felt about that.

KRISTEN HAD HEARD the stories about Jason. How he saved lives over and over again. He was the town hero. But it was one thing to hear about him, quite another to watch him in action.

She opened the car door and sat down. Her hand shook as she slipped the key into the ignition. After the excitement of the last hour, she needed time to calm down.

To calm down and to think.

Everything had happened so fast, she couldn't get her mind around it.

The five minutes Jason spent running through that house was an eternity. The smoke and flames spread so quickly she worried there was absolutely no way he would survive. The fire had hopped and skipped across the roof and she could do little but sit on the trunk of her car rocking the child. The girl refused to let go of her even when the EMTs showed up.

He could have died in there. His job was so dangerous and he did this every day. What had she been thinking?

And this thing between them was real. Too real.

She couldn't do it. Watch him leave every day, wondering if he would come home.

Hadn't her mother done that when her father had been a soldier? And then, one day, he hadn't come home.

Tears streamed down her face.

"It's shock." Jason's voice made her jump. She'd left her door open and had just been sitting there.

"I must look like an idiot." She shoved the tears away with the heel of her hand. "I'm tired from being up with Bibi all night," she lied.

"Don't make excuses. You just went through something traumatic. It's never easy. Take some deep breaths."

She did as he asked. Her stomach settled, but her hands still shook. "I didn't go through anything. I just took care of the girl. You put your life at stake for them. You're a brave man, Jason. And you seem to be just fine."

He touched her shoulder. "Hey, we all have our ways of dealing with things. I told you I'm no hero. I tell you what, I'll have one of the guys take my truck back to the station and I'll drive you home. Give me just a minute."

Before she could say a word, he was gone.

It was senseless to argue with him, of that she was certain. And she had no business driving, even though it was only a few blocks.

When he returned she dutifully stood and walked around to the passenger side, where he opened the door for her.

They didn't talk on the way home.

"I thought I would check on Bibi and the pups," he said as they reached her front door. "Jessie can come get me later."

More than anything she wanted to be alone, but that was selfish. The guy had spent the night taking care of her dog, and then run off to save people.

"How about some coffee?" She needed something to do with her hands.

"Hey." He touched her shoulder. "Tell me what's going on."

Turning she faced him. "I was so scared for you. Everything was so hot and the flames burned so quickly. You didn't come out when I thought you should, and they wouldn't let me come in after you. I thought you died," the words came out in a rush.

Brushing her hair away from her cheek, he leaned in. Before she could realize what was happening he kissed her.

Every thought in her head fled as warmth consumed her.

There was something she wanted to say to him. But she could no longer remember what it was.

He lifted his head and she moaned a complaint.

"I smell like smoke," he whispered. "Let me get cleaned up."

That stopped her. "Oh, what about your back? You— Um, we shouldn't—" Words failed her.

"My back is fine. Even Lisa said it looked worse than it really was. Just a few first-degree burns, which she treated."

She gave him her best I-don't-believe-you glare.

Holding up his hands in surrender he said, "I promise to tell you if it hurts. But we are doing this." He paused. "That is, if you still want to. I mean, as far as I can tell, the kissing seems to make all the pain go away."

He winked.

Up on her toes she kissed him, pressing herself into his body. The bulge at her hip made her smile. He didn't seem to care that she looked like some orphaned rag doll from the town of misfit toys. And she sure as heck didn't care what he smelled like.

His hands tightened around her waist. Hers slid up his shirt to the hard abs underneath. The man was an Adonis. The kiss intensified and his tongue flicked across hers.

Sliding a hand down she cupped him. A sharp intake of breath, and he lifted his head. Searching her eyes with his.

She only smiled and nodded. Pulling her with him, he leaned her against the wall. Their bodies pressed hard against each other.

Cupping her breast, he thumbed her hardened nipple. She gasped and he stepped back.

"No." She tugged his T-shirt to bring him back to her.

He smiled as he kissed her. "Are you sure?"

She met his lips to answer his question.

Her hand slipped to the buttons on his jeans and she opened them so that she could touch him.

There was a moment of panic when she wondered if he would fit, he was so large. His thumb grazed her nipple again, and that, too, was forgotten.

"Bedroom," she whispered.

Then she shoved him away and ran.

He chased her and caught her as they tumbled onto the bed, both of them laughing.

"Wait, the drawer," she said.

"I'm not chasing you again." His fingers trailed down her cheek.

"That's where *they* are." She grinned.

His face twisted in confusion and then he laughed. "It's not time for that yet," he said as he unbuttoned her jeans and slid them off.

"But I want you now."

"You have me, Kristen." He shed his jeans and boxer briefs. The man was perfection. And he wanted her. That was all that mattered.

She reached for him, but he tugged her arms to make her sit up. Then he divested her of her shirt and bra. They were naked and for a moment they stared at each other. Normally, she would feel unsure of herself, and try to cover her breasts or slightly plump belly with her hands or a sheet.

But the gleam of desire in Jason's eyes made her feel more womanly and powerful than ever.

Positioning himself on her right side, he feathered tiny kisses from her ear, down her neck to her breast. She squirmed under his machinations, begging him to join her.

He wouldn't listen. His hand shifted lower on her body, and teased her heat. An ache built within her so fast she thought she would cry if she didn't find her release. There was nothing but his hands and lips on her body, and she ached from the desire he created. His finger slid inside her and that was all it took as the world splintered and her body shook with pleasure.

"Jason," she moaned.

For a moment he left her and she whimpered.

Then he was back, feathering kisses over her face.

"Jason," she begged again. "Now, please."

Kneeling on the bed, he lifted her hips. Before he could shift, she locked her legs behind him and slipped him inside her. Her back arched and she moaned with pleasure.

"Slow down." Jason was breathless. "I can't hold on if you don't—"

"Don't want you to slow down." She panted and rocked herself back and forth against him, her body ready to orgasm again.

"Kristen," he groaned.

But she was gone now. Head back, Kristen rode the tide that surged through her body shattering her into oblivion.

The trembling began in her thighs and arms. She was consumed with him and then she moaned as her body erupted in pleasure for a third time.

"Look at me," he ordered.

She did as he commanded. He met her, thrust for thrust. She didn't think it possible but her body orgasmed again.

"Kristen," he whispered.

But she was far away on a cloud of pleasure such as she had never experienced before.

Tender kisses on her mouth and neck brought her back to him. The possessive gaze in his eyes as his body jerked with orgasm was something she would never forget.

So, this is bliss.

5

Jason smiled as Kristen nestled into his side. With her white hair and fresh face, she looked like an angel from one of her Christmas trees. She brought lightness to his soul. But she made love like a wild tigress. That was something he'd never expected from the prim and proper woman he'd been thinking about for several weeks.

Their lovemaking was intense. And that look in her eyes at the end had done him in. He saw it there, the desire and passion, and she had instantly become an addiction. He'd teased her awake twice more and each time their lovemaking was more intense than the last.

Yes, he was addicted to Kristen, and he didn't see a cure in sight.

Jason silently cursed when he noticed the sun was going down. It was his day off, but he had to make sure everything had been filed properly about the fire. He also had to talk to the detective who was helping the arson investigator.

His gut told him the fire at the house, unlike the one at the mansion, had probably been sparked by something electrical in the attic, but it was important to make sure.

He didn't want to leave Kristen, but duty called. He had a feeling deep in his soul that she would find some way to put up her shields again. The nice, polite Kristen would return, and he would lose her somehow.

He'd seen the way she'd looked at him. She wanted him, but she'd also been hesitant at first—almost as if she had wanted to run away.

But he didn't know why.

If he were honest with himself, he would admit the idea of her running away terrified him.

Man, you've got it bad.

Most of his life he'd put up the same kind of walls Kristen did. That was no longer the case. He cared about this woman. For weeks he'd tried to ignore his feelings. More than once he'd told himself it was nothing more than sexual attraction. They hadn't said more than five words to each other before the other day, but he'd wanted her from the first day he met her.

She was a beautiful woman and so good. He'd seen her work with those women on the committee. Wooing them with her kind words and positive attitude. She brought nothing but goodness.

Still, was this all happening too fast?

He glanced at the clock on the nightstand.

Time to go.

Gently, he shifted his arm out from underneath her and moved off the bed. They had showered after their last bout and changed the sheets, which had been ruined by soot.

It didn't seem right to go without at least leaving a message.

I'll see you at the committee meeting tonight. Plan on dinner. —J

Bibi gave a slight whine as he went to check on her. He let her outside and made sure her food and water dishes were filled. She settled back in with her pups, who were hungry. Bibi nudged them in the right direction.

"Good girl," he whispered as he patted her head.

He heard Jessie pull into the driveway.

He unplugged the Christmas tree and the coffee pot. He really did need to talk to her about the danger of leaving things unchecked. Then he smiled.

His protective instincts had kicked in again.

Yes, he was most definitely in trouble.

H<small>E WAS GONE.</small>

Kristen snuggled into his pillow and held it tight to her. That had been one amazing night. One she would never forget.

And one she could never repeat.

As much as it made her heart ache, she had to stop this craziness. She couldn't get involved with a man who spent his life in danger. Last night she'd been seduced into forgetting.

No, that wasn't true at all. He hadn't seduced her. In fact, she'd been the one who initiated every bit of it.

Like I could keep myself from the best piece of man candy I have ever seen.

As far as she was concerned, this was all Jason's fault. If he weren't so good-looking she would be able to keep her defenses up. She'd grown great at that. Showing a happy face, but keeping the real her tucked deep inside. He'd brought out the wild child within.

She found his note. Dinner. Somehow she would make it through the committee meeting. Then she would make it clear to him that they could not continue.

Best to make the break now before their hearts were entangled.

Keep telling yourself that.

Hours later at the gala meeting, she found herself distracted. Jason wasn't there.

"Kristen?" the mayor's wife asked. "Do you have the guest list complete? Maribel wants to make sure the security at the door has the names."

The security at the door knew everyone on the list. This

was a small town. "Yes, they are updated on the list daily," Kristen said politely.

He'd said he would be at the meeting but he wasn't there.

Was there another emergency? Was he at a fire? Could his life be in danger?

A pounding began behind her right eye and nausea churned her stomach into a sea of worry. She could not take another minute of this.

"It's getting late," she said to the group. "Miss Agnes has to be back at the home by six if she's going to make it in time for Bingo. And Lila, you said the mayor would be angry if you were late to his council meeting."

The mayor's wife might be a bit of a busybody and often used her husband's title to get what she wanted—but she never bit the hand that fed her.

"Quite right," Lila said as she closed her notebook. "It's obvious Kristen has everything under control."

Kristen stifled a snort. That was the first kind word the woman had said about or to her. Until that moment everything she had done, every idea, was wrong. The rest of the women had been wonderful to her, even though she was an outsider. Lila had treated her like a servant, and she was the one who had brought Kristen in.

But Kristen had worked with people in Manhattan who were three times as bad as Lila. It took some maneuvering but Kristen almost always got her way.

"That's what I've been saying all along," Miss Agnes huffed. "She's a bright girl and knows more about this than the rest of us combined."

Kristen reached over and squeezed the older woman's hand.

"Meeting adjourned," Lila said quickly.

Miss Agnes was Kristen's new best friend.

"Do you need a ride back to the assisted living center?" Kristen asked the elderly woman.

"Oh, no, sweet girl. I have a date with Grady O'Keefe. He's picking me up. We're going to eat some cheeseburgers at the Sonic before we head for Bingo."

"Well, you have a lovely time." Mr. O'Keefe was at least ninety and had no business behind a wheel. People on the sidewalks ran into buildings when they saw his old Lincoln coming down the street.

Outside, she waited with Miss Agnes until Mr. O'Keefe arrived.

After running over the curb and screeching to a stop, the old man jumped out of the car like he was twenty and opened the door for Miss Agnes. They were so cute together.

After her last relationship, Kristen had given up on finding her happily ever after. Her former fiancé said he believed in monogamy when he put the engagement ring on her finger, but he hadn't. Six months after that relationship ended, she decided she would marry her career. She'd quit her job as a corporate party planner and gone freelance.

She'd moved from Manhattan to her mother's home in Pine Crest because she wanted a change. The house was an old Victorian and her mother had never sold it because it reminded her of a Norman Rockwell painting. Pine Crest was quaint if nothing else.

There hadn't been much work at first in the small town. Most of her events had been baby and bridal showers, birthdays and bar mitzvahs, but she loved planning personal events. Word spread, and it hadn't been long before she found herself planning one of the biggest events in the town's history.

Her career was really taking off and she didn't have time for a relationship.

Jason would understand. He was as devoted to his job as she was hers.

Where is he?

Her cell rang as she turned on the ignition.

"So, are you going to tell me about your hot night?" her friend Callie asked. "Mandy Rawlins says she saw the fireman leaving your house this afternoon. Said it was the second time he'd been there in twenty-four hours. And why am I hearing this from Mandy and not you?"

"Hey, Callie, sorry. It's been a hectic day. And there's not a lot to tell." She pulled onto the street and put her phone on speaker.

"Oh, that does not sound good. You have that weird tone in your voice. The 'after David' tone. Was he mean to you? Was the sex bad? He's so dreamy, it would be sad if that's his fatal flaw," her friend said.

"Uh, no to both of those."

"Ooooh, then the sex was mind blowing and now you're— Okay, I'm stumped. What is wrong? He's hot. He's great in bed. And from what I know he's one of the nicest guys in town."

Kristen sighed. "He's all of those things. He's perfect. And he's a fireman."

"Again, you've lost me."

She was exhausted, and she didn't feel like talking about Jason. Callie would call her crazy, and she would be correct. But she had to protect herself.

"Oh, no, lo-sing sig-nal." She made her voice sound like the phone had cut off and hit End.

It immediately rang again, but she didn't answer.

A bottle of wine, a bath and one pint of chocolate mocha ice cream—maybe not in that order—and she would be a new woman.

As she turned into the driveway, she saw a figure hovering in the cold. She grabbed her phone to call 911, but the figure waved and the lights hit his face.

Jason.

Great, just great.

At least he was alive.

6

JASON HELD OUT the pizza as a peace offering. They'd had a rush of calls that afternoon and it was nearly seven by the time he showered and changed. He'd been grateful to miss the meeting, but not about losing time with Kristen.

"I thought we would keep things simple tonight." He grinned, but she didn't return the smile.

"Uh, okay," she said.

He should have known. Something dire was rolling around in that beautiful mind of hers.

"I also have wine?" He held up the sack in his hand.

They were met by a bark.

"Bibi." She dropped her bags on the table and rushed to the dog. "I'm sorry I had to leave you. Your babies are so beautiful."

Jason shook his head. The puppies looked like squirmy black cotton balls, except for one, who was pure white.

"Where is your corkscrew?"

She glanced up as if she had forgotten he was there.

"Drawer next to the fridge." She ducked her head and patted the dog on the head.

She opened the door to let Bibi out.

"Look, Jason."

"Found it." He lifted the corkscrew. "We were lucky."

"Lucky?"

"Yeah. It's Alfredo night at Pizza Garden. They don't make this pizza every day." He opened the box and handed her a piece.

She took it, but put it on a napkin on the counter.

"Listen. You're a great guy, but this isn't going to work," she said in a rush. "I'm sorry."

Jason smiled. He'd called it. She was skittish. What happened last night scared her. She wasn't alone. This was the first time he'd ever thought about making a commitment to a woman, and they'd only just met.

"Are you at least going to tell me why? Was the sex that bad?" He joked because he knew she'd enjoyed it every bit as much as he had.

She faced the backdoor but he could see her reflection. She was close to tears.

"Hey." He dropped his pizza onto a paper towel. "Tell me what's wrong." He moved behind her and turned her around.

She stared down at his toes. "Please, don't make this more difficult. I like you. We had fun the last two days. Well, except for the fire. But I'm just beginning to make a go of my career and that has to be the focus."

"Kristen, you're an amazing woman." He lifted her chin with his fingers. "But you are a terrible liar. Tell me what's bothering you. We can handle it."

She batted those beautiful eyes at him. "This morning happened."

She stepped out of his arms. "I thought you were going to die and it ripped me to pieces. How is that for honesty?"

"It's good. You care about me and I care about you."

"No," she said. "I mean, yes. I care. But don't you understand? I can't be with you. I'd be worried every second of the day that something could happen to you. Today when you didn't show up at the meeting, I thought the very worst. I can't live like that."

Her hands twisted in front of her. "I know we've only known each other a short time and we went on our first date twenty-four hours ago. But I care too much already.

"I've been through this sort of thing with my mother when my dad went off to war, twice. Every day she worried. When someone knocked on the door, she didn't want to answer. Then, one day her worst fears came true. My dad didn't come home. And she hasn't been the same since. I don't want to be that woman. I would drive us both crazy with my insecurities about your job."

That last bit hit him in the gut.

He knew about her father, but emotional backlash hadn't crossed his mind. This was something much deeper than a fear of commitment.

As cheerful as she was, it didn't occur to him that she'd faced real adversity, or how losing her father, the hero, could leave scars.

He'd been an idiot. That worldly look in her eyes when he first met her should have been a big clue. And who could blame her? He did have dangerous job and it did take a certain kind of woman to put up with it. That was one of the reasons so many of his fellow firefighters were single.

Still, he wasn't about to hang his helmet up yet.

"There is a big difference in being a fireman and going off to war, Kristen. Most jobs have dangers. The guy who works in the office building at a desk every day could have a heart attack at thirty. We're highly trained professionals. You don't have to worry."

She shook her head. "Jason, you ran into a burning house with no protective gear on to save that family, and you didn't think twice about it."

"I can honestly say that I have never, ever done that before. It was a special circumstance. What was I supposed to do? Any firefighter would have done the same. There was no way I would leave a mother and child to die. Listen to what you're saying."

She squeezed her fingers to her temples. "What you did was heroic, but I disagree about most doing the same. You're special. It's what makes you who you are—an amazing human being. There are better words, but I can't think straight right now.

"But I'm not brave, Jason. I'm a big coward. I've been hurt one too many times, and I know my limitations. I can't do this. It's better to part ways before we get more involved."

More involved.

He was already in deep. But this wasn't the time to tell her. For once in his life he didn't know what to do. If he tried to push, he knew she'd run, possibly back to Manhattan. This would take a special set of skills, which he didn't have at the moment.

Pleading would do no good.

"I have something for Bibi and then I'll get out of your way," he said finally.

Walking past her, he tried not to notice she smelled like Christmas cookies. "I'll need you to open up the French doors around back," he said as he stepped out into the cold.

A few minutes later he was at her back door with a large box made of plywood, but it had been painted to look like a gingerbread house.

He brought it into the kitchen and carefully sat it next to Bibi and her pups. Then he placed a new fluffy dog bed inside of it.

"This is the front flap. It's hinged so it can lay flat. When the puppies get a little older and start moving around you can pull it up and attach it to these pieces and it will keep them in. Bibi can still get in and out, but the pups will be contained.

Have you thought about how you're going to find homes for them?"

She shook her head.

"Well, it will be at least six weeks, which will give you some time. It's good they didn't come earlier. A lot of times people will rush to buy pets during the holidays and they haven't really thought it through."

"You made them a doghouse?"

"It's not really a house. I designed it. Mike, the EMT you met this morning, built it after they dropped the family from the fire off at the hospital for follow-ups. Working with his hands takes his mind off his day job. And really, it's just a box with some hinges.

"And Jessie and some of the other guys at the station painted it earlier this afternoon. Jessie thought he would surprise me by helping out, which is why it looks like something out of Hansel and Gretel."

He'd wanted something a bit more sophisticated for Kristen, but the rookie had been so excited he hadn't had the heart to tell the man to repaint it.

"Thank you. I can't believe you were able to do all this." She gave him another funny look.

"Like I said, I had a lot of help at the fire station."

He grabbed the pizza box. "You can keep the wine. I like my pizza with beer." Placing half the pie on a plate, he closed the pizza box. "I'm still kind of hungry, so if you don't mind I'll take this." He held up the box.

"You need to get the pups to the doc in the next week or so. They are more fragile than they look. They'll need their first set of shots. And you can help Bibi move them to the box, but don't handle them too much."

The look of confusion on her face was something he'd never forget. "Okay then." He kissed her cheek lightly. "Call if you need help with Bibi and the pups. Take care."

He shut the front door behind him. Women confused him more than the rules of rugby. He had to keep her off kilter, at least, until he could come up with a plan of action to woo her.

As he climbed into his truck, he noticed the curtain on the front window had been pulled back. She watched him. He turned his music up loud and pulled out of her driveway.

But he wasn't looking forward to what he had to do next. At least he had some pizza as a peace-making gesture.

"WHAT HAPPENED?" Kristen said to Bibi, as if the dog could answer. "He just…left. Well, he set up a new house for you and then he left. No discussion. No fighting."

She wasn't sure what she had expected, but it wasn't this.
You're an idiot.
Tell me something I don't know.

She picked up her cell and dialed Callie.

"Yo, what's up?" her friend asked. "I heard you just got a big present delivered."

"I need you," was all Kristen said.

"I'll be there in five," her friend replied, and then hung up the phone.

True to her word, Callie stood at her front door dressed in a sexy black dress with heels. She waved to the car that had dropped her off.

"Were you on a date?"

"Yes. Have you opened the wine yet?" She plowed through to the kitchen and opened the wine. "Holy pigs, what in the heck is that?" She pointed to the gingerbread house.

"He made Bibi and her babies a house."

"Uh, okay. So where is he?" Callie handed her a glass of wine.

After taking a big gulp of the liquid, Kristen sat down at the table.

"I told him that I couldn't be with him and—wait. You

made your date bring you over here? Why didn't you tell me? This could have waited until later. You can't do that to the poor guy."

Callie's eyebrow shot up. "Like you know anything about men. Trust me, with that guy, absence makes his libido grow fonder. Besides, you said you needed me. I'm here. Focus on you, Kristen. When did he give you the dog house?"

Kristen gave her friend a strange look. Why would it matter? "After, I told him we couldn't be together" she said.

"Oh, man. He's so into you."

"No, you're wrong. He genuinely cares about Bibi. He's heroic and wonderful that way. He wouldn't let personal differences get in the way of taking care of a dog and her pups."

Callie's smile grew. "And you are so into him."

"I can't be. He's a fireman. He could die at any moment."

Her friend picked up a home design magazine from the mail Kristen had dropped on the table, and bopped her on the head with it.

"Ouch. Why did you do that?" Kristen rubbed her head.

"To show you that something could fall from the sky and kill you at any moment. None of us knows how long we have. We could step in front of Santa Claus and his reindeer and it could be over like that!" She snapped her fingers. "He's the best man you've ever dated and you sent him away."

Kristen didn't bother to argue. "I knew as soon as he pulled out of the driveway that I had made a colossal mistake. But it's for the best. I can't live every day like my mother did. After dad died, she went nuts."

Callie frowned. "She didn't go nuts, she was in search of answers. That's something most people do when they lose someone they love. Granted, from what you've said, some of her religious explorations were a bit out there, but she's happy now. She found her peace. You said so yourself the other day. You told me you remembered your parents loved each other so much that sometimes you felt like an outsider. At least your mom was brave enough to take the risk."

"Unlike the coward that I am." Kristen put her head in her hands.

"So what are you going to do?"

"What can I do? He acted like it was no big deal. I mean, you've seen him. He could have any woman he wants. I told him why I couldn't be with him. He brought in the doghouse. He kissed my cheek, and then he left. He was smiling when he got into his truck. I think he was glad. Maybe he felt like things were going too fast. But I don't think he was that upset about me kicking him out. He's probably at some bar picking up a girl right now."

The very idea brought bile to Kristen's throat.

Callie laughed. "How can you be so naive? He's a man. He put up a front, that's what they do. But you've wounded his ego with your craziness. It may take some hard work to get him back."

"That's the thing. I know it was dumb to let him go, but like I said, maybe it's for the best."

"So you won't be together." Callic shrugged. "But tell me this. You hear a fire truck in the distance, and you aren't going to worry about him? I adore you, but you are full of crap. You care about him, and that's not going to stop." Callie's honesty hit a nerve.

Every time she heard a siren she would wonder.

"No, it isn't." Kristen wanted to bang her head on the table. "Oh, man. I'm a bigger idiot than I thought."

"Yep," Callie said helpfully.

7

THE PIZZA HAD worked. At least Jason thought it had. Sometimes it was hard to tell. The old man eyed him over his desk at the fire station.

"She needs time," the chief said. "Women have to come around to things. They have to think it's their idea."

Jason rolled his eyes. "Isn't that what they say about us?"

"Yes. But I know what I'm talking about. Do little things that make her life easier. Things she doesn't know about."

"I'm so confused. If she doesn't know I'm doing them, how is that going to help?" Jason couldn't believe he was taking advice from the chief, but the old goat had the happiest of marriages.

"Boy, have you learned nothing from this job? When you do an unselfish deed it comes back to you tenfold."

"I'm telling you, it's the Christmas curse. I was thinking about it on the way over here. She's the best thing in my life, and she doesn't want me. Even though I know she cares about me."

The chief pounded his fist on the desk. "Boy, that curse is a bunch of hooey. Sure, you've had some rough times around the holidays. But so do a lot of people. They don't let it get in the way of doing what they want. Are you really going to let this woman go because you are afraid of some curse?"

Jason bristled. "I'm not afraid of anything. You—I'm not afraid."

"If you say so." The chief drummed his fingers on the desk with his eyebrow raised.

That wasn't true. He was afraid of losing Kristen. Every time he thought about it, it gnawed at his gut.

Jason sat back resigned. "Just tell me what to do."

The chief frowned. "She's in charge of this big shindig. You help make sure it goes according to plan. Whatever she needs, you be there for her, but not in a pushy way. You've been to enough of those meetings to know where the strengths and weaknesses are. Plan ahead, boy. You just need to use that brain of yours."

Jason hated when the old man was right, and he always was.

"THE FLU?" Kristen squawked. She sat down on one of the silk-covered chairs in the gala ballroom. Around her was a flurry of activity as the decorations were going up. Crystal snowflake centerpieces were put in place and holly and ivy added to them. A wild, candy-cane profusion of red-and-white chrysanthemums filled the middle of the snowflake centerpieces like the promise of spring ripe in the icy winter. Overhead, workmen strung up the last strand of soft white twinkle lights between the chandeliers. Each strand boasted silver tinsel sparkling like a snowfall, radiating from the central focal point of the grand tree. A winter wonderland with just the right frosting of color. But even the festive trimmings couldn't make her feel better now. She blinked away tears and her hand tightened around the cell.

"Most of my team is out," said the caterer. "We have part of the order done, but none of the hors d'oeuvres or canapés. The pastry chef and his assistant work in another building and are fine. They have the desserts and pastries done. The meats are prepared, just need to be stuck in the ovens. But the rest is what needed to be prepped and cooked today. I'm sorry, but it is not going to happen." He coughed and it sounded like he had the plague.

What am I going to do? The universe really had been playing wicked games lately. Kristen was ready throw up her hands.

"My pastry chef, Joseph, is on the way with what we have prepared. None of it has been contaminated."

This could not be happening. Party 101 was that the food had to be amazing and there had to be more than enough.

"I'm sorry," he said. "Nothing like this has ever happened before, but this stuff went through my entire staff in one day. Two of them are in the hospital with dehydration."

People were in the hospital, and all she could worry about was how to feed two hundred people with no hors d'oeuvres? Though this wasn't the kind of party where chips and dip would suffice. It was Christmas Eve, folks were dressing up, dusting off their checkbooks. They expected to be fed well.

"No, I'm sorry," she said with genuine remorse. "Take care of yourself. We'll manage on this end." She thanked the caterer and hit the off button.

She was a good cook, but she didn't think she could pull off that much food in six hours. Numbness took over her body. She had prepared for every kind of pitfall except this one. It was Christmas Eve, the restaurants in town would be closing early, and they wouldn't be able to fulfill an order like this.

"What's wrong?" That deep voice that turned her insides to mush invaded her thoughts.

"It's okay, Jason. I'll figure it out." She chanced a glance up at his face. It was a big mistake. Every time she looked at the man her heart tugged and there was this voice that chanted, "stupid, stupid, stupid." She really hated that voice.

"What's wrong?" he asked again.

"The catering team has the flu. I don't have hors d'oeuvres or canapés," she explained.

"I'll take care of it," he said as he pulled out his phone.

"Jason, you don't understand. This is food for two hundred people, no one can help us at this point."

He'd been coming to her rescue all week, though she didn't realize it until earlier in the day.

At the beginning of the week, five of the fourteen chandeliers that were to hang in the ballroom had been damaged. She had called every lighting company in a five-hundred-mile radius and no one had any. Later that evening, five chandeliers had arrived. They were perfect for what she needed. When she'd asked around, no one knew who had sent them.

The big Christmas tree, which was to be the main focal point, had been delayed because of weather. But before she could get to the venue that afternoon she received a message from one of the committee members that there was an even bigger tree, already decorated beautifully, waiting for her.

Miss Agnes found out from the chief that Jason was behind all the last-minute saves. It had accidentally slipped when they'd been at the diner that morning for an early coffee.

"That boy can work magic like no one I know," said the elderly woman. "I heard he drove all the way to the city to get those lights. And that they had used the fire truck to help transport the tree they found. He's a good boy."

Yes, he was a very good boy.

And was never far from her.

"I said, I would take care of it," he insisted gruffly. Then he walked off with his phone. The past week they had been polite to one another. More than once, she had thought about apologizing. She wanted to tell him that it was all a big mistake and that she was a fool. But she lacked the courage.

"It's funny." An old man with a white beard and big belly

sat down beside her. "That we can't always see what is best for us."

"I'm not sure I understand," she said.

Who was this man?

"I should have begun with an introduction," he said as if he had read her mind. "I'm Chris Clausen, the Santa you hired for tonight." He held out a hand and she shook it.

She remembered now. He'd been locked up and blamed for the fire at the Price Mansion, but his attorney had him cleared of all charges. It was Miss Agnes who said she should hire him. It was the least the town could do for all the trouble they'd put the poor man through.

There was something about him that made her feel calmer. She was glad Miss Agnes had made the suggestion.

"And I was just saying that sometimes what is best for us is right before our eyes," Mr. Clausen continued. "But we can't see it because of the obstacles we place there."

He moved his chair slightly and Jason's backside was in full view. Surely the old man couldn't be talking about her favorite fireman.

"I'm sure you're right." She didn't know what else to say. She glanced at her phone. "I better get going. So much to do."

He touched her hand lightly. "It's going to be a beautiful party—magical, I do believe." He smiled and she couldn't help but do the same.

"Thank you."

Jason was still on his phone.

Yes, they would need a little magic to survive this night.

JASON WASN'T A big fan of ties and suits, but the Firemen's Annual Christmas Eve Ball was a formal affair. He also wanted to look his best for Kristen. She had been so stressed the last week.

While she put on a mask of confidence for the committee,

he could see her unraveling, little bits at a time. He couldn't blame her. She had been hit with one drama after another. The universe was definitely conspiring against her. He'd done his best to counteract the trouble, and was exhausted from the effort.

But it had been worth it. He glanced around the room. It was beautiful. Her designs were perfect for the space. Everything glittered. All around him people chatted and smiled, which was always a good sign.

But he couldn't find her anywhere.

"Merry Christmas," a deep voice said from behind him.

He turned to find Santa standing there. At least, the Santa the committee had hired to take pictures with the guests.

"Merry Christmas," Jason said.

The old man stared at him and Jason began to feel uncomfortable.

"Is something wrong?" Jason asked.

"Oh, no. From what I understand you've been a very good boy this year, and you're going to get exactly what you want. That Christmas curse of yours will be broken."

Jason laughed. "So you've been talking with the chief. Sorry Santa, but what I want this year, even you can't bring me."

"Ho, ho, ho." The old man laughed. "I wouldn't bet on it. Just keep doing what you are doing. And if you have a chance to dance, take it."

Jason had no idea what the man was talking about. He hoped that he was more coherent with the guests.

"Ah, it's time for me to take my place." Santa waved a goodbye and headed toward the throne in the winter wonderland Kristen had created.

When Jason turned back to the party he sucked in a breath. Kristen was across the room in a gold dress, looking like a princess out of a fairy tale. Her hair was back to its usual color and piled on top of her head in a mass of curls.

Not a princess, a goddess.

Down, boy.

He took a deep breath trying to calm his body. Every night he'd ached for her. Every time he'd seen her during the week it had taken all of his will to keep from reaching out and touching her. During their last committee meeting she had licked her lips and he'd nearly groaned in front of everyone. He wasn't sure how much more his mind and body could take.

The music swelled and an idea popped into his head. He should ask her to dance.

Moving across the floor like a tiger on the prowl, he went after his prey.

THE MAN WORE a tuxedo like a male supermodel. It wasn't fair, Kristen decided as she watched the heads of almost every woman, and a few men, turn in the room.

Darn you, Jason Turner. Why do you have to be so hot and irresistible?

He was heading her way. She wanted to run, but her feet would not cooperate.

"You're an idiot," her friend Callie said. "If that man wanted in my bed for any reason, I'd jump on him like a bear on honey. If you don't want him, I'll take him. I can't wait to lick—"

"Touch him and die," Kristen said through her teeth as she smiled at some of the guests walking by.

Callie laughed. "Well, hon, you can't have it both ways. You either give him up so the rest of us can play with him, or you take him for yourself."

Oh, I'm going to take him.

Her breath caught as he neared.

"Let's dance," he said holding out a hand. He didn't ask, he ordered.

She liked it.

As they moved onto the dance floor she could hear her friend laughing.

"The party is a great success," he said as his arm wrapped around her waist. "Word is that you've raised more than enough money to get the repairs started and the donations are still coming in."

The response from her body shocked her. Heat from his touch spread like wild fire through her body. If he hadn't been holding her so tightly, she would have stumbled.

"You had a lot to do with it," she said. Her voice sounded much stronger than she'd expected.

"I'm not sure what you mean. I just helped out with the committee."

She touched his cheek with her fingertips. "You did a great deal more than that. Agnes told me about the tree and the lights—and tonight with all of this food. How did you do it?"

He turned her on the dance floor. "I pulled in a few favors with some friends. And the guys at the firehouse are great cooks, as are most of their wives."

"The food is perfect. I thought you had called in a professional caterer."

"Well, for future reference, you won't find a tougher sell than a fireman when it comes to food, at least at our station. The guys are constantly trying to outdo one another. And they know how to make food for large crowds."

"Thank you," she said. Her hand squeezed the one he held. "I could not have done this without you."

"That's crazy. You had it all organized. If I hadn't stepped in, you would have found a way around your problems."

She frowned. "Why? After everything I said to you a week ago. Why would you help me?"

Jason smiled. "If you haven't figured that part out yet, well, I can't help you."

She shook her head. "I don't understand," she said honestly. "I know you are an incredible human being. But you must have limits when it comes to stupid people. I'm not sure I could have been as forgiving if the situation had been reversed."

"Kristen," Jason whispered near her ear. "I'm not altruistic. Trust me when I tell you that I had ulterior motives."

"You did?"

The music changed to a slower pace.

He pulled her tighter. "Yes, I love you."

He loved her. It was so much more than she could have hoped for.

"I love you, too. I'm sorry, I've been such an idiot," she said. "And a coward."

His eyebrow rose. "Don't ever call yourself an idiot again. You are a bright, beautiful and successful woman."

"I haven't been so bright when it comes to you. But that has changed. That is, if you can forgive me. I want to be with you. You're all I—"

Jason's mouth descended on hers before she could say another word. She sank into his kiss, and barely heard the whistles and cheers around them.

"We need privacy," Jason said urgently against her lips.

"There is a great little cupboard where we were storing some of the auction gifts."

"Take me," he whispered.

She did—more than once.

THE END OF the party neared. It had been an amazing night. Jason had the woman of his dreams, and he was not going to let her go.

"How soon can we leave?" he asked.

"I need to make sure the cleaning crew and volunteers are ready, and we should be good to go."

She left his side to make the arrangements. She had wanted

to stay and help out, but he'd convinced the volunteers to force her to leave. She had already done so much for the town and for him. He knew she hadn't slept for days. He wanted her home in bed with his arms wrapped around her. She was the best Christmas present ever. He felt like the Grinch at the end of the cartoon where his heart swells and swells. He had no idea he was capable of caring so much for another person.

He went in search of her coat and purse and had them waiting by the door when she arrived.

"Okay. I'll come by in the morning to make sure everything is back as it should be."

He helped her into her coat. "Let's not worry about that now."

Santa passed them.

"Thank you," she called out to the old man. "You did a wonderful job. I heard nothing but compliments about how miraculous you are."

He turned and smiled at them. "My work here is done. Now I have to get on to my real job."

He took off fast on his chubby little legs.

"He is in a hurry," said Eric, one of the EMTs from the fire the other day. Jason had known him for years, and was glad to see him cozying up to Chloe, who gazed lovingly up at him. Jason had pulled her from the fire, but Eric had saved her life. From the looks of things, she was doing the same for him. It was good. The guy deserved true happiness.

"In an odd way, we credit him with getting us together," said attorney Alana O'Hara, who was next to Police Sergeant Noah Briscoe.

"So do we," said Eric and Chloe.

Jason and Kristen stared at one another and broke out in a laugh.

They watched as the old man climbed into his beat-up pickup truck. He held out a beefy hand to wave at them.

"Merry Christmas to all, and to all a good night," he yelled.

For Jason and Kristen it was definitely a merry night. And for the rest of Pine Crest, it promised more holiday magic and tremendous joy.

* * * * *

REQUEST YOUR FREE BOOKS!
2 FREE NOVELS PLUS 2 FREE GIFTS!

Harlequin® *Blaze*™

red-hot reads!

YES! Please send me 2 FREE Harlequin® Blaze™ novels and my 2 FREE gifts (gifts are worth about $10). After receiving them, if I don't wish to receive any more books, I can return the shipping statement marked "cancel." If I don't cancel, I will receive 6 brand-new novels every month and be billed just $4.49 per book in the U.S. or $4.96 per book in Canada. That's a saving of at least 14% off the cover price. It's quite a bargain. Shipping and handling is just 50¢ per book in the U.S. and 75¢ per book in Canada.* I understand that accepting the 2 free books and gifts places me under no obligation to buy anything. I can always return a shipment and cancel at any time. Even if I never buy another book, the two free books and gifts are mine to keep forever.

151/351 HDN FEQE

Name _____ (PLEASE PRINT)

Address _____ Apt. #

City _____ State/Prov. _____ Zip/Postal Code

Signature (if under 18, a parent or guardian must sign) _____

Mail to the **Reader Service:**
IN U.S.A.: P.O. Box 1867, Buffalo, NY 14240-1867
IN CANADA: P.O. Box 609, Fort Erie, Ontario L2A 5X3

Not valid for current subscribers to Harlequin Blaze books.

Want to try two free books from another line?
Call 1-800-873-8635 or visit www.ReaderService.com.

* Terms and prices subject to change without notice. Prices do not include applicable taxes. Sales tax applicable in N.Y. Canadian residents will be charged applicable taxes. Offer not valid in Quebec. This offer is limited to one order per household. All orders subject to credit approval. Credit or debit balances in a customer's account(s) may be offset by any other outstanding balance owed by or to the customer. Please allow 4 to 6 weeks for delivery. Offer available while quantities last.

Your Privacy—The Reader Service is committed to protecting your privacy. Our Privacy Policy is available online at www.ReaderService.com or upon request from the Reader Service.

We make a portion of our mailing list available to reputable third parties that offer products we believe may interest you. If you prefer that we not exchange your name with third parties, or if you wish to clarify or modify your communication preferences, please visit us at www.ReaderService.com/consumerschoice or write to us at Reader Service Preference Service, P.O. Box 9062, Buffalo, NY 14269. Include your complete name and address.

HB11B